Practising for Christmas

by

Rachael Richey

Practising for Christmas

Cover Art by *RJ Morris*

The Wild Rose Press, Inc.
PO Box 708
Adams Basin, NY 14410-0708
Visit us at www.thewildrosepress.com

Publishing History
First Champagne Rose Edition, 2018
Print ISBN 978-1-5092-2236-0
Digital ISBN 978-1-5092-2237-7

Published in the United States of America

Dedication

To everyone who still looks up at the sky
on Christmas Eve night…
just in case.

Chapter 1

23rd December

Olivia stared down at the body of the man at her feet, and her heart leapt into her mouth. Was he dead? What had happened to him? What was he even doing there? She gently nudged at his leg with her booted foot. To her relief, he uttered a small sound, and she dropped to her knees on the sand beside him. A more detailed look at the surroundings suggested to her he had slipped on the rocks and probably banged his head as he fell. They were certainly very slick with wet seaweed, easy to slip on if you didn't take care. She reached out and gently touched his shoulder.

"Are you all right?" Realising that was probably a ridiculous thing to ask since he was lying unconscious on a deserted beach in the middle of winter, she took a deep breath and tried again. "I mean, I know you're not all right, but can you hear me?"

There was no reply, so she bent down closer to him and gently pushed his hair off his forehead. A bruise was forming above his right eye, and as she touched him his eyelids flickered and his lips moved.

"It's all right. Take your time. I'll look after you." She reassuringly put her hand on his shoulder and watched him closely as he tried again to open his eyes. She could see he was young, probably not much older than she was, with thick dark chestnut hair, and although she tried not to look too closely, a very nice body. He was dressed in jeans and a dark green hoodie and had a pair of rather old trainers on his feet. Not the best footwear to be traversing rocks, she thought. No wonder he had fallen.

She looked around her. But what on earth had he been doing there anyway? Apart from the cottage, there were no other houses for miles, and as far as she could see no vehicles parked nearby. Had he walked here? If so, from where, and why? It was two days until Christmas, and the weather was dreadful.

A slight sound made her turn her attention back to the man just as he managed to open his eyes and stare straight at her. They were very piercing green eyes.

"Hello." Olivia smiled at him. "You're back, then. Do you remember what happened? Did you fall?"

Cautiously the man pushed himself up onto his elbow and sucked in his breath. "Ouch, that hurts." His hand went up to his head and located the lump forming on his forehead.

"Is anything else hurt?" Olivia moved closer. "Anything broken?"

"I don't think so." He struggled into a sitting position and flexed both his legs and arms. "I think it's just my head. Must have caught it on a rock when I fell." He looked up at her. "Have I been here long?"

"I don't know. I found you a couple of minutes ago. I actually thought you were dead."

"Sorry. Must have been scary."

"Don't be daft. You don't need to apologise! I'm just glad you're not dead. You should probably go to the hospital to get that head checked out, though. You may have concussion. I can drive you."

"No, I'm fine." He put his hand up and ran it gently over the lump again. "No real harm done. Thanks for the offer, though."

"Honestly, I think you should get checked. Head injuries can be very dodgy. I've done a first aid course. You might think you're okay, but then later you may just drop dead."

The man grinned painfully. "I'm sure I won't, but thank you for your concern. If you've done a first aid course, maybe you could check me over?"

Olivia looked at him in surprise. Much as she would love to check over this gorgeous young man, she wasn't sure she was really qualified to do so. "I'm not sure. It was only a very short basic course. You know, putting people in the recovery position and stuff. I suppose I could check your eyes and things. Make sure the pupils are dilating properly. And we could put some ice on that head." She shrugged. "If you'd like to come back to the cottage with me, I can do that, but if I'm not happy about it, you really must go to the hospital."

The man nodded. "Thanks. Where's your cottage, then? I didn't see any houses when I arrived."

"Just up the road that way." Olivia pointed vaguely up the beach. "It's not actually mine, I'm just staying there for Christmas."

"Okay." He got up onto his knees, wincing slightly. Olivia held out a hand to help him to his feet, and he took it with a nod. "Thanks. Feel really stupid, actually. No idea how I came to fall."

"Those rocks are very slippery. And I don't think those are the best shoes for rock climbing."

He managed a smile. "Can't say rock climbing was

3

on my agenda when I got dressed this morning. Okay, I think I'm all right. So long as your cottage isn't too far."

"No, just a couple of hundred yards. Would you like to take my arm?" Olivia held out her arm tentatively, marvelling again what a lovely body he had. She looked away, feeling suddenly awkward and hoping he hadn't noticed her staring.

"No, I'm okay, thanks. Just let's not go too fast."

They slowly set off up the beach, Olivia keeping a few feet away from the man yet close enough to catch him should he fall. She glanced sideways at him. As well as the gorgeous body, he was extremely good-looking, with thick, messy, dark-reddish hair, piercing green eyes, and just the right amount of stubble.

How on earth had he ended up unconscious on the beach? She was desperate to ask him but felt it would be better to get him somewhere warm first. They reached the road, and Olivia indicated they should turn right. Almost immediately a small white cottage came into view, nestling among a few trees and overlooking the sea.

The man glanced at it in surprise. "Well, I never noticed that when I arrived. It looks cosy."

"Hopefully it will be." Olivia fished in her pocket for the door key. "I only arrived a couple of hours ago. Haven't really had time to warm it up or anything." She grinned wryly. "It has a wood-burning stove. I shall need to work out how to use that."

The man smiled. "You're not from round here, then?"

"No, I live in East London. How could you tell?"

"Well, you've locked the door, for a start. No one

does that round here, and you're obviously not used to open fires. Thought you must be a townie."

Olivia felt her face getting hot. "That sounds so derogatory. I shall cope with the fire. Do people really not lock their doors? That seems a bit unwise." They had reached the cottage, and she inserted her key in the lock and pushed the door open. "If you did that in London, you'd come home to an empty house."

"I know. I lived there for a while. Much nicer in the country."

The front door opened directly into the small living room, and the man walked straight over and sank down onto one of the chairs. "Sorry, can't stay upright any longer." He leaned back and closed his eyes. "I'll be okay in a minute."

Olivia looked at him with concern. She was sure he should be seen by a doctor and thought she might have to insist. "Would you like a drink of something? Water? Tea? Coffee?" She frowned. "Maybe you should have brandy. That's good for something."

"Do you have some?" He glanced up at her.

"No."

"Good job I'd rather have a cup of tea, then. Milk and two sugars, please. And thanks for your help."

"No problem. I'll just put the kettle on. Then I'll check to see if you're okay or not." Olivia shrugged off her jacket onto a chair and kicked her wellies into the corner. "I haven't even had time to investigate the kitchen yet."

She walked into the tiny kitchen that led off the living room and saw at once it was fairly well equipped and even had a slim-line dishwasher built in. She smiled at the sight of that, then filled the kettle and switched it on.

The man was lying back with his eyes closed again, and she hesitated for a moment in case he had gone to sleep. Then, remembering her first aid training, she walked over and spoke to him.

"Try and stay awake. I do remember that's quite important when you have a head injury. How does it feel?"

He opened his eyes and sat up a little straighter. "Sore. My head's thumping, actually. Do you have any painkillers?"

"Yeah, but first I really need to check your eyes. If you need to go to the hospital, I probably shouldn't give you anything just now."

"Go on, then, but honestly I'll be all right. It's not the first time I've bumped my head."

"You were lying unconscious on a beach." Olivia knelt down in front of him. "That's a bit more serious than just bumping your head." She pulled her phone out of her pocket and turned on the torch. "Close your eyes. Right. Cover them with your hands, to make it really dark. That's right. Now when I say, you must open them, and I shall shine the torch at them to see if your pupils change. Right. Are you ready? Now."

He opened his eyes, and Olivia moved really close and shone the light directly into them. His pupils immediately went very tiny, and he put up a hand to ward off the light. Olivia turned off the torch.

"Okay. That seemed to be all right. I think we need to try and get that lump on your forehead to go down. I'll see if there's any ice or anything cold." She got to her feet and went back into the kitchen to look in the fridge. Luckily it was turned on and the freezer compartment had a full ice tray in it. Hunting in a drawer, she found a tea towel, then emptied the ice tray out onto it and folded it into a parcel shape. This she carried back through to the living room and handed to the man. "Hold this against the lump on your head. It should help to make it disappear and hopefully lessen the pain."

He took it with a slight smile and held it tentatively against the visibly throbbing lump on his forehead.

"That's cold. So do I need to see the doctor?"

Olivia sat down in the armchair opposite and watched him closely. "You probably should, just to be sure, but your eyes are doing what they're supposed to, and if we can get the lump to go down a bit, maybe you'll be okay. You shouldn't be alone tonight, though. Where do you live? Can I give you a lift home?"

The man shook his head. "No, thanks. I'll be fine. I'll just rest here for a few minutes, if I may. Then I'll get going."

Olivia stared at him in surprise. "You most certainly will not," she said firmly. "I didn't see a car parked anywhere here, and I don't think you should be driving anyway, and if you think I'm going to let you walk out of here with a head injury, on a cold December afternoon, you have another think coming. In fact, if that's the way you're thinking, I shall take you to the hospital whether you like it or not."

The man stared back at her. "And just how do you propose to do that?" he asked, amusement sounding in his voice. "You can't force me to go. Or to stay here, either."

"I'm pretty resourceful." Olivia got to her feet. "How's your head feeling now?"

He held the ice pack away from his forehead, and she peered at it. The lump was still visible, but she thought it had reduced in size a little. The area around it was red and raw, and she could see a dark bruise beginning to form.

"Does it look any better?" He put up a hand and touched it gently.

"A little. Keep the ice there a bit longer, and then I'll see if I have any antiseptic cream to put on it. It's quite grazed, as well as bruised. If you promise not to walk off into the night, I'll get you some painkillers, too, and that cup of tea."

He grinned at her. "All right, it's a deal. A cup of tea would be nice, and I do still feel a bit wobbly."

Olivia went back into the kitchen, made two cups of tea, and found a packet of painkillers in her handbag. She took two out and carried them and the teas back into the living room. He had lain back and closed his eyes again, and she quietly put the cup down on the coffee table next to him.

"Take these." She held the tablets out. "They may help a bit. Where do you live? Is it far from here? I'll run you home when you feel a bit better."

He opened his eyes and took the proffered tablets. "Thanks. I'll go to a hotel. I guess you can run me there, if you like."

"A hotel?" Olivia sat down and cradled her tea in both hands. "Why not your home? You really shouldn't be alone tonight."

"I'm not going home." He glanced up at her. "I'll hardly be alone in a hotel."

"You know what I mean. And I doubt you'll find one with any vacancies, this close to Christmas. The ones that are open will be fully booked."

She watched him curiously, wondering what his story was. He had been lying unconscious on a beach in the middle of nowhere, was reluctant to accept her help, and was refusing to go back to his house. Maybe he didn't have one. Maybe he was homeless. Although if he was planning on going to a hotel he must have money. She shivered and took a sip of her tea. She really ought to do something about lighting the fire.

The man popped the tablets into his mouth and washed them down with his tea. "Thanks for these. And for all your help." He smiled at her. "Are you staying here on your own?"

"Only tonight." Olivia smiled back. "I have some friends coming tomorrow. We're spending Christmas here. I've come a day early to get the place ready. Warm it up, that sort of thing."

"You drew the short straw, then?" He grinned.

"Not really. The house belongs to my aunt, so it really had to be me. I guess I should have a go at lighting the fire in a minute. It's getting a bit cold in here."

"I'll give you a hand, if you like. I'm used to woodburners."

"Oh, no, don't worry. I wouldn't want to put you out. I'm sure I'll manage. You just rest."

"Nonsense. I feel guilty enough being here. At least let me help you light the fire. Then I'll get going."

Olivia took a swig of her tea and watched him over the rim of her mug. "And where exactly are you going, then? I already told you you shouldn't be alone tonight. Do you have a friend you could go to? I'm happy to drive you anywhere."

The man sighed. "To be perfectly honest, I don't really know where I'm going." He glanced over at her. "Long story, but I left home early this morning in a hurry and didn't bring anything except my wallet and phone. I shan't be going back there, so I guess it'll have to be a hotel."

"You didn't seem to bring a car, either," Olivia observed, leaning back and taking another sip of tea. "Did you walk here? Is your house close?"

"Not really. I walked for a bit, then hitched a lift. I had no idea where I was going and somehow ended up here." He shrugged ruefully. "Decided to go for a walk on the beach to clear my head, and you know the rest."

Olivia watched him for a moment, her mind buzzing with questions she knew she couldn't ask. He was clearly running away from something or someone, and she wasn't about to pry. If he wanted to tell her he would, and since she didn't even know his name, she really had no right to ask. She smiled across at him. "I'm Olivia. I guess it's time we introduced ourselves."

The man nodded. "It probably is. Nice to meet you Olivia. I'm Adam." He reached out his hand to her, and she shook it with a laugh.

"Pleased to meet you too, Adam. I wish it could have been in happier circumstances. How are you feeling now?"

"A bit better. I think the ice has helped. Thanks. Now you must let me help you with the fire."

She looked at him thoughtfully. "Well, maybe you could advise me. I can do it, but you can tell me what to do. Then you can stay resting."

Adam smiled at her. "It would be much quicker if I just did it," he said, getting carefully to his feet. "It won't take me a minute, and you can watch so you know what to do next time. I'm all right, honestly." He moved over to the fire and knelt down in front of it. "In fact, if we do this right and you have the correct fuel, we may be able to get it to stay in overnight. You'll be glad of that if this weather keeps up."

Olivia followed him across the room and squatted down beside him. "I'm sure you shouldn't be doing this, but if you really insist, thank you."

"Right, you seem to have a nice pile of kindling all ready, that's good, and a good pile of logs. This is the type that will take coal as well. I wonder if you have any of that?" He looked around. "That would make it easier to keep in overnight."

Olivia stood up again. "I'll take a look around. There's a little shed in the garden. There may be some there. Can you get it going without coal, though?"

"Of course. No problem. Some matches would be useful, though, and maybe a firelighter?"

Olivia stared at him in consternation. She hadn't given matches a thought, having very little use for them in her flat. "Oh. I'll have a hunt around for some. Hang on." She went back into the kitchen and pulled open the nearest drawer. It was full of cutlery. She moved on to the next one, and to her delight it housed not only a large box of matches but also a brand new packet of firelighters. She picked them up and laughed. "We're in luck. There's both in here." She took them back to the living room and handed them to Adam. "Are these okay?"

"Perfect. Right. If you'd like to go and check for coal, I'll get this set up. Luckily, it's been left clean."

Olivia watched as he opened the door of the stove

and started to arrange some sticks on the grate. What a peculiar day this was turning out to be. First she'd found a beautiful unconscious man on the beach, and now he was in her living room lighting the fire for her! Not at all how she had expected the day to go. At least it hadn't given her much time to dwell on Chris, anyway.

She shook her head to rid her mind of the image of her cheating boyfriend and headed towards the back door in search of coal.

The cold wind whipped around the corner of the cottage as Olivia stepped out into the garden. Shivering, she hurried to the little wooden shed that was tucked into the corner, pulled open the door, and peered inside. It housed a motley assortment of ancient gardening equipment, a couple of very cobwebby deckchairs, and rather strangely, a deflated children's paddling pool, but no coal. She closed the door firmly and ran back into the comparative warmth of the cottage, shivering as she re-entered the kitchen.

"Sorry, no coal." She shrugged apologetically to Adam and knelt down on the floor beside him. "Does it matter too much?"

"Nah, we'll cope. This wood is lovely and dry, actually, which makes it much easier."

She peered around him and saw he had already got a small fire going with the kindling and a firelighter and was about to add one of the larger logs. "Oh, I was supposed to watch you doing that, so I know what to do next time."

Adam glanced at her, amusement in his eyes. "Do you really not know how to light a fire?"

Feeling mortified, she shook her head silently and

looked away. "No. Afraid not. I've never lived in a house with a fire before. Even when I was a kid. How useless am I? I wouldn't survive very well in the wild."

Adam placed another log on the fire and laughed. "Well neither would I, if I can't even keep my feet on a slippery rock." He glanced over his shoulder at her. "We make a good team, actually. I can keep us warm and you can keep us healthy. Your first aid skills would be very useful in the wild."

As Olivia watched him tending the fire, she thought of the many ways he could keep her warm, none of which involved the lighting of a fire. She stifled a smile and turned away, pretending to examine one of the cushions. He really was extremely attractive, and his proximity was quite distracting. He even smelled nice despite the fact he'd spent quite some time lying in the sand.

She sneaked another look at him and wondered what she was going to do with him. She was very loath to let him go to a hotel so soon after his accident and felt she should really be insisting he go to the hospital. She was sure he would be resistant to that suggestion, but other than that she could only come up with one option.

He clearly wasn't going to agree to go back to his own house, so she would have to invite him to stay the night. At least then she could keep an eye on him. Or on his head, at least. It might be nice to have someone else in the house too. She had never intended to be spending the night alone, but since the debacle with Chris, there hadn't been time to get anyone else to come with her. She had to admit she found the prospect of a night alone in a remote cottage more than a little unnerving, so to know there was another person in the house would actually be quite a relief.

She watched as he loaded more logs onto the fire, closed the door, and sat back. He smiled over at her.

"There you go. That should be toasty warm all evening now. Can't have you freeze before your friends get here."

"Thank you so much for that. It already feels much nicer in here. I think it's going to be quite cosy soon."

Adam got to his feet and put out a hand to steady himself on a chair. Olivia leapt up and was at his side in an instant.

"You're still dizzy. You must sit down. I knew I shouldn't have let you do the fire." She took his arm and held it until he sank down onto a chair and closed his eyes.

"I'm okay." He leaned back and rested his head. "Just stood up too quickly. Could probably do with a bit longer rest before I go, though. If you don't mind?" He opened his eyes and stared up at her.

"You're not going anywhere." Olivia perched on the arm of the chair and watched him with concern. "I already decided that. You must stay here tonight. It really wouldn't be right for you to be on your own, and if you're still refusing to go home, then you must stay here. There's plenty of room. Then I can keep an eye on you."

He watched her silently for a moment, then closed his eyes again. "I really ought to protest, but to be honest, I haven't got the energy. I'm actually beginning to think you may be right about not being on my own. But I don't want to impose." He opened his eyes again and looked at her solemnly. "And you have no idea who I am. For all you know, I could be a serial killer looking for my next victim."

"You could be," Olivia agreed. "I just have a gut feeling that you're not. I can't help feeling a serial killer wouldn't have been stupid enough to get stranded unconscious on a beach with only his wallet. They're usually a little more organised."

Adam raised his eyebrows. "Maybe it's all an act. Maybe I was pretending to be unconscious to get you to take me to your house."

"And the huge lump on your head?"

"Self-inflicted."

"Ah. Right. Well, in that case you're even more stupid than I initially thought." She stood up and moved over to the fire, holding out her hands to warm them. "But it is true that I know nothing about you, and I'm quite sure my mother would have a fit if she knew I'd invited you to stay, so how about you tell me a bit about yourself?"

"How do you know I won't lie?"

Olivia looked over her shoulder at him. "I don't. I'll take that chance." She turned round and curled up on the sofa, watching him. "I'll tell you a bit about me too."

Adam nodded slowly. "Okay. Seems fair. You go first."

"No. You go first. It was my idea, and it's my house."

He gave a bark of laughter. "Okay then. My full name is Adam Richard Munro, and I'm twenty-seven."

"Right. I'm Olivia Jayne Marshall, and I'm twenty-five. And a half."

"I had a dog called Rascal when I was ten."

"That's not really very helpful." Olivia looked at him severely. "How does that tell me if you're a serial killer or not? What happened to it?"

"I killed it with my bare hands, then buried it in a shallow grave with my baby sister and my grandmother."

"It's possible this experiment won't work." Olivia felt her lips beginning to twitch. "You need to take it more seriously if you want the chance of a bed for the night."

"It was your idea to offer me a bed. I'm quite happy to leave now and take my chances with the weather and the head injury." Adam smiled angelically at her, his eyes twinkling.

"Hmm. Fair enough. I suppose this was my idea." Olivia sighed. "Okay then. I wasn't supposed to be here alone tonight. My boyfriend was supposed to be with me."

"What happened to him? Is he buried in the garden?"

"I wish!" Olivia couldn't help a little giggle. "No. We broke up yesterday." She paused, then glanced up at him and sighed. "I caught him snogging someone else at a Christmas party."

"Ah. Sorry, that must have been hard."

"It was…" She searched for the right word. "Annoying, more than anything. Now everyone will turn up tomorrow and think I've failed at yet another relationship."

"Does this happen often, then?" Adam raised his eyebrows in surprise.

"Well, no, not the same thing, obviously. I've just not got the best track record when it comes to relationships, and this one…" Olivia paused, wondering how much to say. "This one had lasted nearly three months. I thought we'd manage to make it through Christmas, at least."

"You don't sound too upset about it."

She glanced at him and wriggled uncomfortably. "I guess I'm not. He had a lot of faults, and to be honest, we didn't have a lot in common. But I just wanted the others to see I could hold down a relationship too."

"Who are the others?"

"My best friend Jess, her boyfriend Tom, and Sarah and Jon. Jess, Sarah, Jon, and I were all at Uni together, and Sarah and Jon have been going out for like…forever. They hadn't even met Chris. Now they'll think I made him up or something."

"Well, they can't be very good friends if they'd think that." Adam shrugged. "Don't worry about them. And it's Chris's loss."

Olivia looked at him awkwardly. "Thank you. But this isn't really helping me decide whether or not you're a serial killer. Now you know far too much about me, and I know nothing about you apart from your name."

"And age."

"And age. Now, come on. Where do you live? Why won't you go home? I've told you personal stuff, so it's your turn."

Adam leaned back and closed his eyes again. "Okay, I guess I ought to tell you. I really don't want you thinking I'm some sort of criminal." He opened his eyes. "I live about twenty miles away. This morning I got back from the shops, where I'd been doing some last-minute Christmas shopping, to find my girlfriend in bed with my best friend. So I left."

"Oh, god, I'm sorry." Olivia looked at him sadly. "That's even worse than my story. That must have been a dreadful shock." She paused. "Is it your house?"

"Yes."

"You should have told them to leave, not left yourself."

"I should have killed them both and buried them in the garden, but to be honest, I wasn't really thinking straight." He smiled ruefully at her. "Hence the arrival on your beach with only my wallet and phone, and the wrong footwear."

"So you don't want to go back? Do you think they'll still be there?"

"Maybe." He shrugged. "I rather expect she'll try and talk her way out of it, so yes, she probably will still be there. That's why I'm not going back."

Olivia nodded. "Okay. All the more reason to stay here, then. Unless you want to take her back?"

"No."

"What about your parents? Where do they live?"

"Mum lives in Paris and Dad in San Francisco. My sister is off travelling in Europe for a year, and my grandparents are on a cruise."

Olivia stared at him and burst out laughing. "Oh, I'm sorry! It's dreadful of me to laugh, but that does sound funny. A real jet-set family you have. My parents live in a semi in Romford, and my sister's a nurse in London and working over Christmas. The nearest my grandparents have ever been to a cruise is a pedal boat at Southend!"

Adam gave a wry grin. "I guess it does sound a bit grand. Dad made a lot of money when he was young.

Then when they divorced, Mum married some guy who owns a chain of hotels in Europe. But it must be nice to have parents who are still married to each other."

"It is." Olivia smiled. "And right now I'm beginning to wish I was spending Christmas with them."

"What would you be doing?"

"Well, tonight Mum will be rushing around madly baking things we really don't need, and shouting at my dad to keep his feet off the furniture. Tomorrow she'll spend all day preparing the veg for Christmas dinner, and rushing out to the shops at least three times for things she's forgotten to buy or suddenly decides she needs. She won't actually sit down and relax until after lunch on Christmas Day, when she'll fall asleep on the sofa watching whatever ghastly film is being inflicted on the world."

"So will it just be them this year, then?"

"Oh, no. My grandparents will be there, and my aunt Janice. Possibly her boyfriend, if he's out, and their best friends from down the road."

"If he's out?" Adam looked at her curiously.

"Aunt Janice doesn't have the best taste in boyfriends. This latest one has just done a stretch for possession. I think he's due out today or tomorrow, though."

"And you were worrying I was a criminal." Adam chuckled.

"He's not related to me." Olivia frowned at him. "She'll dump him soon, I'm sure."

"So what else do you want to know?" Adam stretched his long legs out in front of him and yawned. "I'm six foot one, weigh twelve stone…"

"I don't need to know that," Olivia interrupted him with a giggle. "I'm certainly not telling you what I weigh. Are you hungry?"

"I guess I am a bit."

"Me too. I'll see what I can rustle up. I brought some food with me, but most of the Christmas food is coming tomorrow." She got to her feet. "We've got all the basic stuff here now, though."

"What time are your friends arriving?"

"Not sure. I think Sarah and Jon said something about midday. Jess has to work, so she and Tom will be later."

"I'll make sure I've gone by then." Adam looked up at her. "It's very kind of you to let me stay, especially as you think I'm a serial killer. It's very trusting of you."

Olivia pursed her lips. "Yeah, well, the jury's out on that right now. We'll have something to eat, and I'll make a final decision about you after that."

She moved into the kitchen and leant against the worktop, staring out the window. The trees outside were being buffeted by the strong breeze blowing in off the sea, and tufts of white spray were flying in and landing on the glass. She took a deep breath.

What on earth was she doing letting a complete stranger stay the night in a remote cottage with her? The business about the serial killer was a joke, of course, but he really could be anyone. She sneaked a glance back into the living room and saw he had leaned back and closed his eyes again. The lump on his forehead had gone down a lot, but it was being replaced by a huge purple bruise that was threatening to engulf his eye as well.

He really was extremely good looking, and Olivia couldn't help wondering just how much that had to do with her offer of a bed for the night. She shook her head in annoyance. Of course it didn't have anything to do with it. She was genuinely worried for his health and really felt she couldn't let him spend the night alone. He didn't look dangerous. In fact, he didn't look capable of very much at the moment. She peered at him more closely.

"You're not asleep, are you?" she called.

"No. Just resting my eyes."

"Good. Stay awake as long as you can." She turned back into the kitchen and set about rustling up a meal for them.

****

"That was lovely." Adam laid down his fork and smiled at Olivia. "Really nice."

"Thank you. You're welcome." She stood up and picked up their empty plates. "I have some chocolate biscuits, if you'd like some pudding?"

"No, I'm fine, thanks. But I'd love a cup of tea."

"No problem. How's your head feeling now?"

"Still throbbing, but a bit better." He grinned at her. "Don't worry. I'm not going to drop dead."

"Probably not, but I'm not taking any chances." Olivia looked sternly at him. "You need to take this more seriously. You were actually unconscious, and neither of us knows how long for." She put the plates down again, her face serious. "In fact I know you should have gone to the hospital, and that's why I'm being so fussy about it. If you die, it'll be my fault. And I don't even know you."

"It won't be your fault." Adam got to his feet with

a grunt. "Firstly, it won't happen, and secondly, if you remember, I refused to go to the hospital, and left to my own devices I would have gone to a hotel." He looked down at her with a lopsided grin. "Letting me stay here is very kind, and actually the best thing you could have done. If I drop dead—which I won't—then it will be my fault, not yours."

"Well, that's a great relief." Olivia looked up at him, very aware of his proximity. "But you must make sure you really *don't* drop dead, because I might have a hard job explaining your cold stiff body when my friends arrive."

"I'll make sure." His eyes were sparking with amusement, and he grinned again. "It would make for an interesting conversation, though."

Olivia picked up the plates again and walked into the kitchen. "But one I'd rather not have. You stay there. I don't think you should walk around too much."

"I was actually wondering where the bathroom is." He was hovering in the doorway.

"Oh, I'm sorry, I never thought. It's up the stairs, first door you come to."

He disappeared up the steep, narrow staircase, and Olivia put the plates into the dishwasher. She was fairly sure he wasn't a criminal, and was inclined to believe his story of the unfaithful girlfriend, but she would be glad when the night was over. Not least because she was finding it slightly unnerving to have such an attractive man in the cottage alone with her. Not that he'd be interested in her, of course, as he was obviously upset about the girlfriend, and anyway, he was way out of her league.

She straightened up and opened the chocolate

biscuits. Chris had been reasonably good-looking, in a very ordinary sort of way, but nothing on Adam.

Olivia bit into a biscuit and closed her eyes. The way his hair flopped over his forehead was most distracting, as were his piercing green eyes. She had never seen such compelling eyes, actually. They were most unusual.

She heard him come out of the bathroom and flicked the kettle on ready to make some tea. Glancing at the clock, having completely lost track of time, she was surprised to see it was already well gone nine. She made the tea and carried the mugs into the living room as Adam sank back down onto the chair.

"Are you okay?" Olivia placed his mug on the coffee table and watched him with concern. His face was very pale, and he had closed his eyes.

"Yeah. Just a bit sore, and surprisingly wobbly."

"Do you feel sick at all?"

"No. Don't think I could have managed that enormous dinner if I felt sick." He opened his eyes and smiled at her. "No, I'll be okay. Bit tired, too. It's been a long day."

Olivia sat down opposite him and took a sip of tea. "I guess so. I hadn't realised how late it was either. I'll sort you out somewhere to sleep in a minute." Her mind flicked around the other rooms in the house. There were three bedrooms upstairs: one for her, one for Jess and Tom, and one for Sarah and Jon. She supposed Adam could have one of them, but then she'd need to re-do the bed before the others arrived. She glanced up to find him watching her.

"I'll sleep on the sofa," he said. "I'm sure you have the bedrooms ready for your guests, and it's actually very cosy down here."

"Are you sure?" Olivia raised her eyebrows. "I could sort out a bed…"

"I'm sure." He smiled at her again. "Don't fuss. It's warmer down here, as well. Easier to get my dead body out in the morning if I'm downstairs, too."

Olivia giggled. "Very good point. No need to make it more difficult for myself, is there? Okay then, I'll see if I can find you a pillow and a blanket or something."

She located the necessary items in a small cupboard in one of the bedrooms and quickly made him a makeshift bed on the sofa.

"Thank you, that looks very comfy." She found he was watching her, an amused look in his eye.

"No problem. What's so funny?"

"Nothing."

"You look like you're laughing at me." To her horror, Olivia felt her face begin to flush, and she turned away to rearrange the pillows again.

"I just think it's very sweet the way you insist on mothering me." Adam gave a little chuckle. "You've totally taken charge."

"Well, if you won't look after yourself, then someone has to do it." She turned and raised an eyebrow at him. "It's your own fault. Now, you know where the kitchen is, if you need a drink or anything. I think I'll go up to bed now, and you look like you could do with a sleep."

"Oh, I'm allowed to sleep now, am I?" Adam stood up and smiled down at her.

"You may." Olivia returned the smile. "I think it's been long enough. I may pop down in the night and wake you up, just to make sure, though."

"You'd better not!" Adam laughed. "I'm not at my best when I get woken unexpectedly. Now off you go, and I'll see you in the morning."

Olivia turned and started up the stairs. "Okay, sleep well."

"Olivia? Thanks again for this. You didn't need to do any of it. You've been very kind."

She glanced over her shoulder. "As I said, no problem." She continued up the stairs and pushed open the door to her bedroom. The small room felt chilly after the warmth of the woodburner in the living room, and she shivered. Here was she, freezing upstairs, while her guest, a complete stranger, was tucked up all warm and cosy in her living room. Something wasn't right there!

She smiled to herself as she got ready for bed, still finding it hard to get her head around the events of the day. First she'd found an unconscious man on the beach, then she'd invited him to stay the night, knowing almost nothing about him. And he was, quite honestly, the best-looking man she had ever seen. She pulled on her pyjama trousers and sat down on the bed.

If she'd met him under normal circumstances, at a party or something, somewhere where they were both fully conscious, she knew full well she would have been tongue-tied and awkward around him. As it was, she had, as he had pointed out, taken charge and not found time to be her usual shy self. Maybe rescuing wounded men was her forte. She might have to consider a career change.

With a grin, she slid under the covers and lay down. What a strange day. And tomorrow was another problem. She knew Adam would insist on leaving, and to be honest he probably had to, but she still couldn't help worrying about him. And she had to admit she would be sorry to see him go. They'd probably never meet again.

Her eyes flitted over to the door. Despite the fact that she believed his story about the girlfriend, she couldn't be absolutely sure he wasn't a serial killer, and there was no lock on the door. Imagining what both her mother and Jess would say to her, she jumped out of bed again and carefully pushed a chair against the door, wedging it under the handle. Just to be perfectly safe. She nodded to herself, then slid back into bed and turned off the light.

Chapter 2

Christmas Eve

"Good morning."

Olivia stepped off the bottom stair as Adam appeared in front of her, holding out a steaming mug of tea.

"Good morning. Thank you." She smiled at him. "You made it through the night, then?"

"I did. And you may have noticed I didn't murder you, either."

"Yes. I was pleased about that." Olivia took the tea and moved over to sit down on the sofa. "I'm pleased you're not dead either, of course."

"Yeah. Me too." Adam perched on the chair opposite her and took a sip of his tea. "And my head feels much better this morning."

"Glad to hear it. Did you sleep okay?"

"Like a log. It was lovely and warm."

"Unlike my bedroom." Olivia grinned wryly. "Ironic, really."

"I'm sorry."

"Not your fault. There doesn't seem to be any heating upstairs. Maybe the whole house will warm up when we've had the fire lit for a bit longer." She glanced over at the woodburner. "It's still very warm. Did it stay in overnight?"

"Nearly. It was still glowing. I just added a bit more to get it going again properly. Should last for hours now."

"Thank you." Olivia looked at him in surprise. "You didn't need to do that."

"Nonsense. Least I could do after you being so nice to me. Can I get you some breakfast? I see there's some bacon in the fridge."

"No, I'm fine with the tea, thanks." Olivia shook her head. "But you can have some, if you like."

"I've had some toast. That'll do me. I'll get going in a bit, leave you to get ready for your friends."

"No rush." Olivia felt her heart sink as she realised she would probably never see him again. "They won't be here for ages yet. Where are you going anyway?"

Adam drained his cup and leaned back in the chair. "Not sure. Probably to a hotel until I figure out what to do about Naomi."

"Will you forgive her?" Olivia watched him intently, wondering why his answer mattered to her.

"No. Not a chance." He glanced over at her. "It's not the first time she's had a little fling. She persuaded me it was just a mistake, the first time, and I thought things were all right. So, no, she's had her second chance."

"I'm sorry. You must be very upset."

Adam shrugged. "Not as much as I would have expected. I think I never felt as close to her after the first time, really. She's been dropping hints about getting engaged recently, but it just never felt right. Now I know why." He sighed. "So now I have to get her out of my house. Can't really do that on Christmas Eve, so I shall keep away for a few days."

"You could stay here…" Olivia tailed off as she realised that probably wouldn't work.

"No, I'm fine. You have a full house. I wouldn't want to intrude on a group of friends anyway. But thank you for the offer. You've done more than enough already." He smiled at her again, and she felt her stomach do a little flip as his hair flopped over his forehead. He pushed it back with a wince as his hand brushed against the lump. "Hmm, that's still sore, then."

"D'you want some more painkillers?"

"Maybe in a bit."

Olivia finished her tea and put the mug down on the coffee table. "Thanks for the tea. What time is it anyway?"

"Nearly ten. Are you sure your friends won't be here yet? I really should leave before they arrive."

"Bit early yet. I'm guessing not until at least half eleven or twelve. Time for another tea first." Olivia got to her feet and picked up the mugs. "The weather looks a bit wild out there today too. Obviously I'll give you a lift to the nearest town when you're ready to leave."

Adam followed her into the kitchen and leant against the worktop while she made the tea.

"No need. I can call a taxi."

"That would cost a fortune!" She glanced over her shoulder in surprise. "Especially today. No, honestly, it's no trouble. I'm sure there'll be something I need to get from a shop anyway. Not used to being this far from civilisation."

"I must say, from my time living in London, I didn't find that very civilised." Adam gave a short laugh. "Far more civilised in the country."

"Well, you know what I mean." Olivia handed him his mug. "All my life I've lived a few yards from a shop and surrounded by houses. This all seems quite alien. And way too quiet." She laughed, suddenly feeling a little self-conscious. "You were right, I *am* a proper townie."

"Be good for you to spend a few days here, then." Adam raised his eyebrows. "Do you like it so far?"

"Well, I was enjoying the beach until I nearly fell over your body." She grinned up at him, cradling her mug in both hands. "After that, I can't say I've really taken much notice of my surroundings."

"Fair point." Adam grinned. "You must make sure you go back to the beach while you're here, though. It's worth a look. Don't you ever go on holiday to country places?"

"Not really." Olivia shook her head, beginning to feel a little under scrutiny. "When I was a kid we used to go to Southend, and since I've been going with friends, we usually go somewhere like Spain. So always very busy and built up." She shrugged. "I suppose you've been all over the place, have you?"

"Pretty much." He nodded. "We've lived all over, actually, and before my parents split up we had a place in London and a couple of holiday homes, so I've experienced everything."

Olivia watched him as he spoke, trying not to let her eyes linger too long on his lean body, covered only with a thin T-shirt and jeans. He was so much more attractive than Chris, or indeed any of her previous boyfriends. Naomi must be a very stupid girl if she didn't appreciate what she had. As she lifted her mug to her lips, there came a loud knocking on the front door.

Olivia jumped and stared at Adam in consternation.

"God, who on earth is that? It's way too early for Sarah and Jon."

"I'll go." Adam put down his mug and moved towards the door. "Just in case it's another serial killer."

Olivia's eyes followed him as he walked over to the door, unlocked it, and pulled it open. To her horror, she saw the smiling faces of Sarah and Jon staring at him in surprise.

"Oh! Hi, I'm Sarah. You must be Chris." Sarah reached out and grabbed Adam's hand, shaking it warmly. "Wow, Liv never said you were so good-looking." She laughed and glanced at her companion. "In fact, I owe Jon a fiver. I bet him she'd invented you and that she'd be here alone." She peered over Adam's shoulder to where Olivia was lurking behind him. "Sorry, Liv! Just going by your track record."

Olivia stepped forward. "This isn't…"

"…the place to discuss this." Adam cut in and stood aside. "Come in. Pleased to meet you. Would you like a cup of tea? It's pretty cold today."

As they entered the house, Olivia moved next to Adam and glared at him. He winked at her and ushered the newcomers into the living room.

"Tea would be nice." Sarah stood in the middle of the room and unwound her long scarf. "It's lovely and warm in here. I did wonder if it would be a freezing hovel, but it looks quite nice."

Olivia bridled a little. "This is my aunt's cottage. Why would it be a hovel? In fact, why would I invite you to stay in a hovel? Now, take a seat, and we'll get you some tea."

"Unless you have wine?" Sarah sat down and

shook her long blonde hair back. "That would be even better."

"God, Sarah, it's only just gone ten." Jon looked apologetically at Olivia and Adam. "Sorry about her. I think she's still drunk from last night, actually. Tea will be great, thank you."

Olivia followed Adam into the kitchen and pulled him into the corner.

"What on earth are you doing?" she hissed. "Why didn't you say who you were?"

He grinned at her. "You heard what she said. They assumed I was Chris, and then when she said that about thinking you'd made him up…well, I couldn't let her get away with that. She's not your best friend, is she?"

"No. No. Jess is my best friend." Olivia shook her head. "But that's not the point. Now what do we do? Are you going to stay all over Christmas and keep pretending to be Chris? How the hell is that going to work?"

Adam grinned again. "I think it could. You just tell me a bit about him, and I can act the part. After all, they haven't met him, so it doesn't really matter what I'm like. And I'm obviously much nicer than he is anyway."

"And better-looking," Olivia muttered darkly. "That's why you did it, isn't it? Because she said how good-looking you are. God, men are so shallow!"

"I was actually trying to be nice. I thought it would save your feelings. I could see her making a big thing out of the fact that he wasn't here, and making your life a misery." He reached out and took her hand. "Come on, this could be fun. What d'you say?"

Olivia stared at him, acutely aware of the touch of his hand on hers, and realised it could actually be rather fun pretending to be Adam's girlfriend. She dismissed all the obvious problems from her mind and managed a small smile. "Okay. We'll do it. Sarah was being rather a bitch, wasn't she? Can't let her get away with that." She took a deep breath. "Jess is another problem, though. She hasn't actually met Chris, but I did describe him to her. We may have to let her into the secret."

"Well, I hope she's nicer than that one out there." Adam jerked his head towards the living room. "Can't say I think much of her so far."

"Jess is lovely. I forgot what a bitch Sarah can be sometimes. She's not always like that, though. And Jon is very nice. Okay, let's make this tea, then. We'll sort everything out later."

Adam smiled at her. "Great. So you get to keep an eye on my head for another couple of days, and if I *am* a serial killer I'll have plenty of victims all here ready for me."

"So you will." Olivia grinned at him as she popped tea bags into the mugs. "Maybe start with Sarah, eh?"

He laughed out loud and got the milk out of the fridge. "Okay, no problem if she carries on like that. By the way, what job does Chris do? And how old is he?"

"He's twenty-eight, his surname is Booker, and he's a data entry processor." Olivia poured the boiling water into the mugs.

"What the hell is that?"

"No idea. I suppose he processes data."

"That sounds ghastly. Can't he have a more interesting job?"

"Well, he hasn't. He's not very interesting."

"Do they know what he does?"

"No. Jess does, but they don't."

"Right, well, he's just changed his job. He's now a computer programmer."

"That doesn't sound any better."

"Believe me, it is." Adam picked up two of the mugs of tea and grinned at her. "And I can answer questions on that. Trust me, I'll be believable."

Olivia followed him back into the living room where Sarah and Jon had made themselves comfortable on the sofa. Sarah looked up as they came in.

"I moved that bedding. I hope you don't mind. Did one of you sleep in here, then?" She was watching them, her eyes speculative.

"Oh, that was me." Adam spoke smoothly, handing her a mug. "Liv was snoring so badly I couldn't stand it any more, so I came down here."

There was a moment's silence, and then Sarah burst out laughing. "Seriously? Liv snores? That's epic."

"He's just kidding you, Sarah." Olivia handed Jon his tea. "Tell her why it really was…Chris."

His lips twitched, and he shrugged. "Okay, fair enough. I had a little accident yesterday, banged my head, and I couldn't sleep. I came down to get some painkillers and stayed so as not to disturb Liv."

"How did you bang your head?" Jon was looking at Adam closely. "That bruise on your forehead looks sore."

"It is." Adam sat down next to the fire. "I slipped on the rocks when we were taking a walk on the beach yesterday."

"Oh, is there a beach here?" Sarah looked over at the window. "We must go and see it."

"Of course there's a beach." Olivia stared at her in amazement. "You knew this was a seaside cottage. Surely you noticed the sea when you arrived."

"She was too busy texting." Jon gave Sarah a playful slap on the leg. "She misses a lot of things."

"I knew the sea was there." Sarah sniffed in annoyance. "I just didn't know there was a beach."

"So what do you two do, then?" Adam was watching them curiously.

"God, Liv, haven't you told him about us?" Sarah tossed her hair back and crossed her long legs. "I work for a fashion magazine, and Jon is a data analyst."

"Right. In London?"

"No, Jon and I live in Birmingham. Liv, didn't you tell him anything?"

"We had other things to discuss." Olivia looked at her, trying to recall why she'd invited her. She didn't remember that Sarah had been that self-obsessed last time she'd seen her. "Would you like to see your room? Then you can bring your things in and get unpacked. Jess and Tom won't be here until later. Jess has to work." She stood up. "Come on, I'll take you upstairs. Chris and I will pop out to the shops while you do that. I wasn't expecting you quite so early, and we were hoping to have done that before you arrived."

"Oh, we'll come!" Sarah's face lit up. "I love shopping."

"No, not that sort of shopping. Just a few oddments we forgot for the meals. You two get settled in, and we won't be long." She led the way up the stairs and opened the door of the bedroom next to her own. "This is your room. Sorry it's a bit cold. We're hoping the heat from the woodburner will filter up here eventually."

"It's lovely." Jon squeezed past her and walked over to look out the window. "And look, Sarah, there's the sea."

Sarah tutted loudly and joined him at the window. "I know. I just didn't know there was an actual beach. Okay, let's get unpacked, then. And we have food to bring in, too. Can we have wine when you get back?"

"Maybe. Let's see what time it is, shall we? Right. See you in a bit. Help yourselves to more tea if you like." Olivia turned and ran back down the stairs to where Adam was waiting, a puzzled look on his face.

"Why are we going shopping?"

"Dear god, do I have to think of everything? What do you have with you?"

"My wallet and phone."

"Right. No clothes, then? No toothbrush? No Christmas presents for anyone, even me? I think we need to shop if we're going to make this believable."

Adam had the grace to look a little sheepish. "Good point. Come on, then, there's a huge supermarket not too far away. We can probably get everything from there."

Olivia pulled her coat on and wound a long woolly scarf around her neck. "Okay, then, let's go. Have you got your wallet? 'Cos I'm not paying for your clothes. You got us into this situation."

"That's fine. I have plenty of money. Lead on." He pulled the door open and stood aside for her to go through.

Her car was parked around the side of the cottage, and as she unlocked the doors and slid into the driver's seat, Olivia glanced at Adam. "By the way, I prefer

Olivia. Sarah always calls me Liv, and so do the others sometimes, but I really prefer Olivia."

"No problem." Adam nodded as he fastened his seatbelt. "I prefer that too. I only called you Liv because Sarah did, and I wanted to make it look like I knew you."

"Fair point." Olivia chuckled as she reversed out onto the road. "I guess we should try to look as though we're acquainted, since we're supposed to have been going out for three months."

"I suggest we use this little outing to get to know each other better." Adam was watching her as she drove. "I don't want to get caught out with any awkward questions." He pointed to the right. "Turn here. That supermarket I mentioned is a couple of miles along this road."

Olivia followed his directions, and within a few minutes a small town came into view, a large supermarket sprawling on the outskirts. She turned into the car park and found what appeared to be the last remaining space.

"Oh, god, I forgot what a nightmare shopping would be today." She sighed as she turned off the engine. "If you didn't need some clothes, I'd suggest we didn't bother."

"Well, I really do." Adam pushed open his door and stepped out into the car park. "I can't really spend the next few days in the same clothes. Probably ought to get a razor, too."

"Oh, you don't need to do that." The words were out of her mouth before Olivia could stop them, and she looked away in embarrassment. She had noticed as soon as she saw him how well his stubble suited him and had been trying not to let her eyes be drawn to his face too often. Now he'd realise what she meant. She locked the doors and, keeping her head down, headed towards the entrance. "Come on, let's get this over with."

Adam fell into step beside her, and she could feel his eyes on her. She glanced briefly up at him and found he was grinning at her.

"There's no rush, is there?" He shrugged. "I'm in no hurry to get back to Sarah, anyway. I thought we could have a coffee, and you could tell me things I ought to know, as your boyfriend."

"A coffee?" Olivia looked up at him. "What, you and me? Here?"

"Yes. You and me." Adam was watching her with amusement. "Who else did you want to invite?"

"No, I didn't mean..." Olivia tailed off, not actually knowing what she had meant. God, she must be sounding really stupid. She was surprised he even wanted to continue with the silly deception. "Okay, then. I guess I'm not in a hurry to get back to Sarah either. Do they have a Costa here?"

"They do." Adam caught her elbow and steered her across the shop towards the Costa concession. "What would you like?"

"Hot chocolate would be nice. Thank you." She smiled at him and followed him up to the counter. "Are you going to have something to eat?"

"I wasn't, but you can if you like."

"Maybe a brownie?" Olivia glanced up at him guiltily. "If you don't mind?"

"Of course I don't mind. You can have whatever you want. Why don't you go and get a table while I order?"

Olivia moved over and slid behind a small table in the corner. She unwound her scarf and hung it with her coat over the back of the chair. She was still reeling from Adam's actions at the cottage and was wondering just how his little plan was going to work. Hundreds of potential problems were hammering on her brain, and she was beginning to feel slightly out of her depth.

"Here you go. One hot chocolate and one brownie." Adam deposited the tray on the table and slid into the seat opposite her. "Right. Time to get to know each other."

"We did that yesterday."

"Yeah, right. I know you used to go on holiday to Southend, and you think I'm a serial killer." Adam lifted his coffee mug and watched her over the rim. "I think we need to do better than that. I don't even know what job you do. It may only be for a couple of days, but if we're going to make the others believe we've been going out for three months, we need to get our stories straight."

Olivia sat back in her chair and sighed. "I know. I guess you're right. But I honestly don't know what you were thinking. There are so many ways this could go wrong."

Adam grinned at her. "I know. Fun, isn't it?"

He looked so much like a naughty schoolboy that she couldn't help smiling back. "I hope so," she said with a chuckle. "Right. Let's see what we can do. I'm twenty-five, my birthday is in June, and I live in East London."

"What do you do for a job?"

"I'm a teacher. At a smallish primary school in

South Woodford. I teach Year Three."

"Really? I'd never have guessed that." Adam was watching her with interest. "I put you down for working in an office."

"I have one sister, who's twenty-eight, two parents, who live in Romford, and as I mentioned before, an aunt with very bad taste in boyfriends." She glanced up at him. "Chris has met my sister but not my parents or aunt. My sister is called Claire. They didn't hit it off."

"Why not?"

"Basically because Chris is a bit of an arsehole." Olivia gave a wry grin. "But please don't think you have to behave like that. Even if you are a serial killer, you've got much better manners than he does."

"I gather you're not too upset about his behaviour, then?"

"Not really. Certainly not surprised. Just annoyed at the timing, really." Olivia took a bite out of her brownie. "You've met Sarah and Jon, so I don't really need to tell you much about them, but Jess is my best friend. She's a buyer for Harrods and very good at her job. She hasn't been going out with Tom for long, about six months, I think, but he's very nice. I think you'll like him."

"So how come your best friend hasn't met your boyfriend?"

"Just timing, really. Jess and I try to meet up once a week for a girly natter, so obviously no boys allowed, and we've both been so busy the last few months that we haven't managed a full double date at all. I have described him to her, though. We may have to improvise a bit there."

"Do I look anything like him?"

"No. Not really. He has dark hair, but it's not reddish like yours. And his eyes are brown. You're about the same height, but that's all."

"And I'm better-looking."

"Yes." Olivia rolled her eyes. "Yes, you're better-looking."

"Right. I understand why none of them have met him, but surely in this day and age they will have looked him up on Facebook or something?"

"You'd think." Olivia nodded. "He does have Facebook, of course, but he's one of those annoying people who don't put pictures of themselves. His profile picture is some dreadful footballer. No idea who. And he just doesn't put photos on. I guess there are some that his friends have put there, but you'd really have to search. Jess doesn't have the time for that, and Sarah is far too self-obsessed to care."

"Yeah, about that. She doesn't really seem your type."

"She's changed since we left Uni." Olivia sighed and took a drink of her hot chocolate. "She was always a bit selfish, but she seems to have got worse lately. She can be nice, though."

"I'm sure she can." Adam smiled at her. "Well, I probably know enough about you to get by, but what about me? Or rather what about Chris? What do I need to know there?"

"Well, I told you he's twenty-eight and a data entry processor. He lives in Romford in a crummy flat. He has one brother, who's twenty, and still lives with his parents. I haven't met any of them. He loves football and supports West Ham."

"Well, I think you had a lucky escape there." Adam

41

drained his coffee cup. "He's not nearly good enough for you. Right. I shall try and remember all that, but as I told you, he's changed his job. He's now a computer programmer. I think he may have gone off football a bit, too."

Olivia giggled. "I used to hate the football talk. Never understood a word of it." She looked at him curiously. "Are you a computer programmer? Is that why you want him to be one?"

"Sort of." Adam shrugged. "I work in computers, anyway. And I can programme. Easier to sound knowledgeable if anyone asks. Okay, I think we have enough to work with there. Are you ready to shop now?"

"Yeah, let's get it over with." Olivia got to her feet and pulled her jacket back on. "I'm afraid you'll have to get me a Christmas present. It might look odd if you didn't. I shall get you one too. It doesn't need to be anything fancy or expensive."

"I shall get you a present suitable for the occasion." Adam grinned down at her, his green eyes twinkling. "I suspect he would have wanted to impress your friends."

"You really don't know him," Olivia muttered darkly, winding her scarf around her neck. "He's very selfish. I had to remind him to get any presents."

"Should I get them for the others too?"

"No. I've got stuff for them that we can give as joint presents. From us both."

"So are you going to give me the one you bought for Chris, then? I hope it's not a football shirt."

"Heaven forbid!" Olivia giggled and followed him back into the shop. "No. You wouldn't like what I got him. And I didn't bring it anyway. I'll get something else for you."

"Okay, well, tell you what, why don't we split up for a bit. I'll get my clothes and your present, and you can get my present and any other bits you need, and we can meet up again in, say, twenty minutes?"

"You can clothes shop in that time?"

"I'm a boy." He grinned at her again. "See you back here, then?"

Olivia nodded and watched as he walked away towards the clothing department. He really did have the most gorgeous body, and she was fascinated to see what he would look like in different clothes.

Or no clothes at all. That would be even better. She smiled to herself. She could dream, couldn't she? At least she got to pretend to be his girlfriend for a few days. Weird though the whole affair was, it could turn out to be quite fun. He seemed to have a good sense of humour, and she could imagine there would be some interesting moments in the days to come.

She looked around her for inspiration for a present to get him but had no idea where to start. It must be something suitable for a boyfriend, but nothing too expensive or intimate. She wandered over to the aisle with the DVDs and CDs in. If she knew what sort of music he liked, she could have got him that. Or even if he liked films. She realised he knew a whole lot more about her than she knew about him.

With a sigh, she wandered along the aisles looking for ideas, very nearly deciding to buy him a bottle of wine, when she came across the books. She paused and scanned along the shelves. Maybe there was something there that would spark an idea. After a moment her eyes fell on the perfect gift. She picked it up and, with a grin spreading across her face, read the back cover. It was exactly right, and if she had read him correctly, he would appreciate the joke. With a chuckle, she headed straight for the checkout so she could have it hidden in a bag by the time he joined her. She grabbed a roll of wrapping paper on her way past and carried them both to the self-service checkouts.

She had been waiting by the magazines for about five minutes when Adam joined her, his hands full of bulging carrier bags.

"You found some clothes, then?" Olivia raised her eyebrows.

"I did. Not too bad a choice, actually, for a supermarket. I think I've got every possible social occasion covered."

He looked so pleased with himself that Olivia burst out laughing. "You do know we're spending the next few days in a tiny cottage with four other people, don't you? No fancy parties, or whatever you're used to."

"Just wanted to be prepared. How was I to know if you lot wore evening dresses and tuxedos on Christmas Day? People are unpredictable. And I got casual stuff, too."

"You bought a tux in a supermarket?" Olivia stared at him in amazement.

"Well, no. But I got some smart stuff. Do I need a tux?"

"No. No, of course you don't. You'd be better getting sweat pants and pyjamas, if I know my friends."

"Well, as I said, I'm now prepared for anything. Did you get what you wanted?"

"Yeah. It was just a present for you, actually." She couldn't help a grin spreading over her face.

"What? Why are you laughing?"

"You'll find out. Shall we go?"

"We could, but can I just ask you something?"

Olivia looked round at him. "What?"

"I couldn't help noticing you didn't have any decorations in the cottage. Christmas decorations. Is one of your friends bringing some?"

"Oh. No, I don't think so. I completely forgot about decorations. Do you think we need some?"

"Of course. It's not Christmas without decorations. And a tree. Let's go and get one. Come on, I know just the place." He headed towards the door, and Olivia ran to keep up with him.

"Wait!" She caught his arm as he stepped out into the car park. "Are you suggesting we get a Christmas tree?"

"Yes."

"What, like a whole, real, tree?"

"Well, what sort do you usually have? Half a one?"

"No, don't be silly. But we're only in the cottage for a few days. What will we do with a tree afterwards?"

They had reached the car, and as they loaded the bags into the boot, Adam glanced at her.

"You have a point, I suppose. It could be awkward deciding who takes the tree home. Maybe we could just get a tiny one? You know, in a pot? And lots of decorations." He grinned at her. "Come on, it'll be fun."

With a reluctant grin, Olivia got into the driver's seat and started the engine. "Okay, then, where are we going?"

"Just up the road. It's a garden centre. They have

the most amazing selection of decorations and trees."

"How do you know all this?" Olivia reversed out carefully and headed towards the exit. "Is this very near where you live?"

"It's not far." Adam's face was expressionless. "Close enough for me to know the shops, anyway. There, turn left out of here, and first right."

As they parked in the garden centre's enormous car park, Olivia looked at Adam. "Why are you doing this?"

"What d'you mean? Buying a Christmas tree?"

"All of it. Why did you care if Sarah was going to take the piss because Chris wasn't there? Why do you care about us having decorations?"

He turned to face her, his expression serious. "You rescued me yesterday. You were very kind. You let me stay in your house even though you had no idea who I was. That was very brave!" He grinned. "Or very stupid.. It just seemed like I owed you a kindness too. Something just snapped when Sarah made that comment about betting you'd invented the boyfriend, and I acted without thinking. The decorations, on the other hand, are essential. You can't have Christmas without them, so stop complaining and over-analysing everything, and let's go and get some!"

Olivia got out of the car and followed him towards the shop, her mind mulling over what he'd just said. So he was playing the part of her boyfriend because he thought he owed it to her, not because he liked her. Or anything. Not that she really thought he did. She glanced at him as he walked through the door ahead of her. It would have been nice, though.

"Coming?" Adam looked over his shoulder at her

and held the door open. "The trees are this way. Let's get that first, then look at the decorations."

Olivia smiled at him. "This is quite fun, actually. Haven't been shopping for a Christmas tree for years. Not since I was a kid." She followed him through the shop and out onto a patio area that had a selection of trees, netted and leaning against the wall. "These are huge! We can't have one of these."

"Come this way." Adam caught her hand and pulled her past the large trees and around a corner. A little row of smaller trees, planted in pots, was lined up. They were disappearing fast and Adam went straight over and pointed at one. "How about that one?"

Acutely aware that he was still holding her hand, Olivia stared at the little tree. It was about eighteen inches tall, and a very nice traditional tree shape. She smiled up at him. "Looks nice. How much is it? Sometimes these places are very expensive."

"That doesn't matter." Adam let go of her hand and bent down to pick up the tree. "Don't worry about the money. I'm paying. Now let's go and get the decorations."

Before she could protest, Olivia found herself being shepherded back into the shop and down the stairs into what could only be described as a Christmas grotto. The whole floor seemed to be covered in lights, tinsel, baubles, and a whole feast of decorations of a kind she never even knew existed. "Wow!" She stared around her in fascination. "This is awesome. I could get to quite like Christmas if I spent time in here."

"You don't like Christmas?" Adam looked at her quizzically, collecting a basket and beginning to fill it with tinsel.

"It's all right. I just think too much is made of it. It's far too commercial, and it's always the same at our house. Really boring."

"That's a shame. It can be a magical time, if you let it. Come on, choose some baubles for the tree. We need lights, too. We can string them around the room."

Olivia watched as Adam sped around the shop, tossing items into the basket, occasionally glancing at her with a wide grin. He was in his element, and she realised it was going to be a lot of fun getting to know him better. It was just a pity it was only for a few days.

Maybe they could keep in touch afterwards. She shook her head. That would be too much to ask for. It was enough he was helping her not to lose face with her friends, but it was only because she had rescued him on the beach. He felt he owed her something. They would have no reason to stay in touch. He'd probably sort things out with his girlfriend anyway.

The thought made her unaccountably depressed, and she turned away pretending to study a little model train that was running around a snow-covered model village, the little houses lit up with fairy lights.

"That's nice." Adam appeared at her side. "Shall we get that too?"

"What, the village?" Olivia stared at him in surprise. "It's really expensive, and to be honest, although I like it, I can't see it appealing much to Sarah and Jon."

"Probably not." Adam nodded. "Why did you invite them? No, sorry, not my place to question you. I'm not even supposed to be here." He grinned at her. "I think we have enough. Shall we go? We can have fun this afternoon putting them up before Jess arrives."

Chapter 3

"There you are!" Sarah looked up from where she was lying on the sofa, wine glass in hand. "You've been hours. We had to start on the wine."

"*You* had to start on the wine." Jon appeared at the kitchen door. "Don't bring me into it. You *were* a long time, though. Where have you been?"

"Getting a Christmas tree." Adam held up the little tree triumphantly. "Can't have Christmas without a tree. And lots of decorations. We can put them up this afternoon."

"Great idea." Jon disappeared back into the kitchen. "Kettle's just boiled. Either of you want a coffee?"

"Tea, please." Olivia dumped her bags on the sofa next to Sarah and wriggled out of her jacket. "And something to eat, I think. We should have some mince pies somewhere." She perched on the arm of the sofa, located the bag containing her gift for Adam, and glanced at Sarah. "You did remember to bring the turkey, I hope?"

"Of course. Don't fuss." Sarah uncurled her long legs and stretched them out in front of her. "It's quite cosy in here. How does that fire thing work?"

"It's a woodburner. You have to light it." Olivia got to her feet and headed for the stairs. "Just got to put something in my room. Back in a minute."

She ran up the stairs and hurriedly hid the bag containing the book and wrapping paper under the bed. She'd pop back later and wrap it up ready to put under the tree. Smiling to herself, she ran back down to the living room, realising just how nice it was to have a tree to put the presents under. This was actually promising to be an even better Christmas than she had been anticipating. Thanks to Adam. A complete stranger who was rapidly capturing her heart, and who was currently in the process of setting up the tree on a small table in the corner. He had changed into a new check shirt as soon as they had got back, and she couldn't help noticing how nicely it accentuated his well-toned figure.

"Does this look okay?" He turned to her as she stepped off the bottom step. "Or would it be better over there?" He pointed to the opposite corner of the room.

"It's perfect where it is." Olivia smiled at him. "Thanks for insisting we get it. Can I put some lights on it?"

"Of course. They're in that bag. I got several lots. We can put the others around the room."

"Ooh, look at you two playing house." Sarah chuckled and took a long swig of her wine. "And you're being so nice to each other. No one would believe you've been going out for months."

"Maybe that's *why* we've been going out for months," Adam said smoothly as he wound some tinsel around the little tree. "You should try being nice to Jon sometimes."

"Cheek!" Sarah scowled at him, then curled her feet up under her again and laughed. "You're probably right, though. It certainly seems to be working for you two."

"Of course it does." Adam put out a hand and pulled Olivia closer to him. "And long may it last." He looked down at her, winked, and brought his lips down on hers.

The kiss only lasted a few seconds, but Olivia felt her whole body begin to tingle with desire, and her legs started to turn to jelly. She gripped his shoulders to support herself, and when he pulled back, their eyes locked for a second before he grinned over his shoulder at Sarah.

"See, can't go wrong by being nice to each other. Pass me that blue tinsel, Olivia. I know just the place for that." Silently, her head still spinning, Olivia handed him the long piece of tinsel. He took it from her and gently wound it around her neck, taking the ends up and tying them in a bow on top of her head. "There. Suits you. It matches your eyes. Now take these lights and go and wind them around the banisters." He pulled some more tinsel out of the bag and threw it over to Sarah. "Make yourself useful. That would go well on the banisters too."

With a lazy grin, Sarah uncurled from the sofa and caught the tinsel. She went and sat down on the stairs, watching as Olivia carefully wound the long string of multi-coloured lights around the banister rails.

"Chris is nice," she commented.

"Yes." Olivia didn't trust herself to say more, and bent her head as she fiddled with the lights.

"I reckon he's a keeper."

Olivia plugged the lights into the nearest plug socket and switched them on. "Oh, that works. They look nice."

"Even better with the tinsel." Sarah jumped up and wound the long strand of red-and-green tinsel around the banisters, following the line of the lights. "See, that's lovely."

"Here's some tea, girls." Jon appeared from the kitchen and handed them both steaming mugs. "It's looking great in here. Much more festive."

"Thanks." Olivia took the mug and cradled it in her hands. "I could do with this. What happened to the mince pies?"

"I'm heating them up in the oven. Nicer hot."

"I have him well trained." Sarah walked over and wound her arm around her boyfriend's waist. "He knows I can't cook, so he does it all. He makes a mean cup of tea, too." She took the other mug and sipped it. "I've probably had enough wine for now anyway."

"There, doesn't that look better?" Adam stood back and admired the room. "Can't believe you were going to make do without decorations. Now we have somewhere to put the presents, too."

"I still have one to wrap." Olivia watched Adam as he tidied up the remaining decorations. "I have a whole roll of wrapping paper. Does anyone need some?"

"For once I'm all prepared." Sarah smiled smugly and carried her tea over to the sofa. "Very organised."

"Yeah, because you got the shop to wrap all your presents." Jon chuckled. "You can't take credit for that. Mince pies should be ready now. I'll bring them in here."

Olivia walked over and sat down on the hearth rug in front of the woodburner. "How about you...Chris? Do you have anything to wrap?"

"I'm all sorted, thanks."

Sarah chuckled. "Stop fishing, Liv. I'm sure he's got you something."

Adam finished tidying up the decorations and sat down on the sofa next to Sarah. Olivia watched him as he leaned back and closed his eyes. He was really entering into the make-believe with gusto. She wondered what she should expect next. She shuffled across the floor on her bottom and leaned up against the nearest armchair, wishing Adam had chosen to sit on the floor with her rather than next to Sarah.

"Is your head okay?" She watched him closely.

"Much better, thanks." He didn't open his eyes. "Just a bit tender to touch."

"Mince pies, guys." Jon placed two large plates of hot mince pies on the coffee table, accompanied by a tub of brandy butter and a carton of cream. "Dig in. There's plates and spoons here, too."

"Brilliant." Olivia smiled up at him and crawled across to collect some. "Brandy butter goes so well with mince pies."

"Brandy butter goes well with most things." Adam had opened his eyes, and Olivia found he was watching her, a small smile on his lips. "Do we have Christmas pud for tomorrow?"

"Of course. Well, Jess is bringing it, so I hope so."

"What time are they arriving?" Sarah picked up a mince pie and popped the whole thing in her mouth.

"I think she finishes work at four, so I guess about sevenish." Olivia glanced up. "What time is it now?"

"It's only three. What shall we do this afternoon, then?" Jon perched on a chair and helped himself to a mince pie and cream.

"We could play a game."

Olivia looked at Adam suspiciously. "What sort of game?"

"A board game."

"Do we have any?" Sarah looked around vaguely. "Or did you bring some?"

"No, I didn't bring any. Thought there might be some already here."

"Are there, Liv? It's your aunt's house."

"I have no idea. I haven't been here since I was ten. I'll have a look in a minute."

Adam sat forward and took a mince pie. "Is this the same aunt that has such bad taste in men?"

"Good lord, no." Olivia giggled. "That's my mum's sister. She lives in a flat in Romford. I don't think she's ever been further than ten miles from home. No, this belongs to my dad's older sister. She lives in Gloucester with her rich husband and snotty son, and this is their holiday cottage. She rents it out over the summer."

"Probably are some board games here, then." Adam shrugged. "Holiday cottages usually have things like that."

"There's a cupboard under the stairs." Jon pointed across the room. "Have you looked in there?"

"I haven't looked anywhere yet." Olivia got to her feet and went over to the stairs. "Let's see."

She pulled the cupboard door open and wrinkled her nose. "Ooh, dusty. Bet it's full of spiders, too." She knelt down and peered inside. A small pile of boxes sat in the far corner, and she reached in and pulled them towards her. "You were right. We have quite a selection here: Monopoly, Cluedo, Scrabble, Mousetrap, and Mastermind."

She glanced over her shoulder. "What d'you fancy?"

"I think Cluedo." Adam's eyes were glinting. "Quite fancy a bit of murder."

Olivia grinned, shoved the rest of the boxes back into the cupboard, and carried the Cluedo over to the coffee table. "That okay with you two?"

Sarah shrugged. "Sure, might be fun. Haven't played Cluedo in years. Can I be Miss Scarlet?"

"If you like." Olivia spread the board out on the table. "Right. Choose your pieces and let's have a murder!" She caught Adam's eye, and they grinned at each other.

****

By six thirty they had played three games of Cluedo, of which Adam won two and Olivia one, and were all in the kitchen trying to prepare a buffet supper for when Jess and Tom arrived.

"Ever heard the saying 'Too many cooks...'?" Olivia said with a grin as she squeezed between Adam and Sarah in an attempt to fill the kettle. "Maybe we shouldn't all be in here together."

"Nonsense, more fun this way." Adam vaulted up onto the work surface and smiled at her. "I'll keep out the way up here, if you like."

"How is that out the way?" Sarah reached around him to open the fridge. "I personally think we should let Jon do all the cooking. He's very good."

"Hey, I don't mind doing the turkey, but everyone, even you, Sarah, must take their turn. This is fun, though." Jon pulled two large pizzas out of the oven and placed them on the top. "Think we're nearly done anyway."

"Time for wine!" Sarah peered into the fridge and squeaked in surprise. "This is real Champagne! Did you bring this, Liv?"

Olivia looked round in surprise. "No. I brought a bottle of Prosecco. Can't run to the real thing. Are you sure it's real?"

"I bought it." Adam shrugged. "Thought it would be nice to have some of the good stuff. I got a bottle for tonight and another for lunch tomorrow. Hope that's okay?"

"That is totally awesome." Sarah reached up and kissed him on the cheek. "I told you this one was a keeper, Liv. Can we open it now?"

"Shall we wait till the others arrive?" Olivia caught Adam's eye and raised her eyebrows. "That was very generous of you, Chris. Did you get those this morning?"

"Yeah. Just saw them on the shelf and thought it would be nice." He jumped down from the work surface. "Are we setting the food out on the table? Shall I take some through?"

Olivia went into the living room and opened up the leaves of the gate-legged dining table. She covered it with the cloth she had found in the kitchen drawer and smoothed it flat. "We'll put it all on here, and people can help themselves."

Adam appeared behind her and placed a plate of pizza on the table. "You don't mind about the Champagne, do you?" he asked quietly, his mouth close to her ear. "I thought you deserved a treat."

"It's lovely." She glanced up at him. "You shouldn't have, but it's lovely. They may wonder why you have so much money, though. Remember you're supposed to be a data entry processor."

"No. He changed his job, remember? Computer programmer now."

"Are they that well paid?"

"Well, this one is." He grinned at her and put his arm around her shoulders. "Hope you didn't mind about the kiss earlier. We have to put on a show for them."

"I'll cope." She looked at him solemnly, noting how his eyes were twinkling. "We have to make it believable, of course."

"Oh, god, are you two being nice to each other again?" Sarah came up behind them and deposited a couple of plates on the table. "Early night for you, I think!"

As Sarah walked back to the kitchen, Olivia raised horrified eyes to Adam. They would have to share a room. She hadn't even given that a thought. Last night had been no problem because he'd slept on the sofa, but tonight it would look really weird if he did that again. He smiled down at her.

"Don't worry. We'll work something out. It's a big enough room. I can sleep on a chair or something."

"There's only a small wooden one."

"Well, on the floor, then."

"You can't do that. That would be dreadful."

"How big is the bed?"

"What? Well, it's a double, I guess. Usual size."

"We could both sleep in it and put a pillow between us."

Detecting the hint of laughter in his voice, Olivia looked at him suspiciously. "I don't think you're taking this seriously enough. We only met yesterday. We really shouldn't be sharing a bed."

"Or pretending to be boyfriend and girlfriend, and kissing to fool your friends." He smiled down at her. "But it seems we are. We just need to adapt to the circumstances. Don't worry, you can trust me."

"I know." She looked away, feeling her face begin to get hot. "And I know you're not going to kill me now, either."

"Not you, no." He inclined his head. "The jury's out on Sarah at the moment, though."

"You seemed to be getting on pretty well with her in the kitchen."

"What? When she kissed me for buying the Champagne? That was more to do with her desire for alcohol than with me." He glanced at her in amusement. "Do I detect a hint of jealousy?"

"No, of course not." Olivia turned away in annoyance. "Why should I be jealous? Don't be silly." As she started to move away, there came a loud knocking at the door, and she darted over and pulled it open.

"Livvy! We're here!" Jess tumbled into the room and enveloped her friend in a bear hug. "I managed to get away from work a bit early. This looks lovely." She let go of Olivia and stepped into the room. "It's so cosy and Christmassy."

"Hello, Jess. Hi, Tom. Come on in. It's freezing out there." Olivia stood back to let Tom in. "Supper's just about ready. That was really good timing."

Sarah appeared from the kitchen. "Jess, Tom, great to see you. Now we can open the Champagne." She gave them both a hug and pointed to Adam. "Have you two met Chris before? I expect you have."

"No." Jess was looking at Adam, a slight frown

creasing her forehead. "No, we haven't. Are you Chris? You don't look anything like Olivia described."

"Nonsense." Olivia stepped forward. "Of course he does. I said he was tall and had dark hair. Chris, meet Jess, my best friend, and her boyfriend Tom."

"Pleased to meet you, Chris." Jess shook his hand, still studying him intently. "And I'm sure you said he had brown eyes."

"I doubt I mentioned his eyes." Olivia took her friend's arm and led her nearer the fire. "Come and get warm. Then I'll show you to your room."

"Livvy, he's gorgeous. You never told me that," Jess whispered, glancing back over her shoulder to where Adam was laying more food on the table. "How could you not have told me that?"

"I don't know. Didn't want to brag, I guess. So how was your journey? Did you remember to bring the pudding?"

"Of course I remembered the pudding." Jess took off her coat and shook her dark curls back out of her eyes. "But don't change the subject. Where did you find Chris? Are there any more like him?"

"Jess! What about Tom?"

"Only joking. I'm just gobsmacked at how good-looking he is. And those piercing green eyes. I can't believe you didn't mention those."

"Oh, well, whatever. Now come and see your room, and then we can eat." She led the way upstairs, wondering how she could steer Jess off the subject of Adam's deliciousness without making her suspicious. Maybe they'd have to do a bit more to make it look like they were a couple. More kissing would be good, of course, but she wasn't sure she should instigate that.

Maybe she could cuddle up to him on the sofa or something. That would be fairly innocent. "Here's your room. You have a sea view, but it's too dark to see it just now. It's a full moon tomorrow, though, so if the clouds pass it should look lovely."

"This is smashing." Jess looked around in appreciation. "This could be fun. If everyone gets on. What's Sarah been like so far?"

Olivia rolled her eyes. "A bit annoying, but she's improved since she arrived. She's obsessed with drinking the wine, though. You may want to hide some in your room in case she drinks it all."

Jess laughed. "She doesn't change. I'll just get into something more comfortable, if you don't mind. These work clothes are ghastly. Can I put my pjs on?"

"That's a good idea." Olivia grinned at her. "I may just join you. See you downstairs in a minute. Where did Tom go?"

"I think he was going to bring the food in from the car. I hope he gets on with Chris. It would be nice if they could be friends."

Olivia smiled nervously and sidled out of the room and into her own. She closed the door and leaned against it with her eyes closed. This was going to get even more stressful. Everyone loved Adam, and somehow she was going to have to explain why she suddenly split up with him just after Christmas. They would all think she was mad. With a sigh she wriggled out of her jeans and pulled on her check pyjama trousers. It would be nice to be comfy for the evening.

Before leaving the room, she reached under the bed for the present she had bought for Adam and hurriedly wrapped it. She smiled to herself, imagining his face when he opened it. She hoped she had read his character correctly.

Back downstairs she found Adam, Sarah, and Jon in the living room, and Tom unloading food into the fridge.

"Pyjama party!" Sarah jumped up. "Cool idea. I'll go and get mine on." She ran up the stairs, and Olivia laughed.

"It was Jess's idea. You don't mind, do you, guys?"

"Why would we?" Jon shrugged. "Sarah spends half her time in her pyjamas anyway."

"Is the food all ready now?" Olivia glanced over at the loaded table. "It looks awesome."

"Yep, just waiting for everyone to come back down, and we can open the Champagne." Adam got up from where he'd been adding logs to the fire and looked at Olivia with a grin. "You weren't kidding when you said I didn't need a tux, then?"

She laughed. "I did tell you. I *will* wear clothes for tomorrow's lunch, though."

"Don't bother on my account." He winked at her as he walked into the kitchen. "You look lovely like that."

Olivia looked away and casually plumped up some cushions. She felt her face was slightly hotter than usual and was struggling with the feelings that his presence, and his comments, engendered in her.

"Here we are." Sarah and Jess appeared at the bottom of the stairs, and Sarah looked hopefully at Adam. "Are you opening the Champagne?"

"I am." He appeared in the doorway of the kitchen with the bottle in his hand. "Can someone get the glasses out?"

"Is that real Champagne?" Jess moved over and sat down on the sofa. "I haven't had real Champagne for years."

"Yep. Moet and Chandon."

"Bloody hell, Chris, that costs about thirty-five quid a bottle!" Jon stared at him in surprise. "And you bought two."

Adam shrugged. "It's only Christmas once a year. Here goes." He eased the cork out of the bottle, and it shot forward and bounced off the coffee table. "Ha, good shot. Quick, where's a glass?"

Olivia held out a glass, and he poured the frothing liquid in, his eyes twinkling as he looked at her. She smiled up at him.

"This is lovely. I'm not sure I've ever had real Champagne before. It's a proper treat."

Adam filled the remaining glasses and handed them round. Then he raised his in the air. "To good friends, and new friends. Merry Christmas, everyone."

"Merry Christmas!" they all chorused together, and Adam reached over and clinked his glass with Olivia's.

"Specially to new friends," he murmured, taking a sip and watching her closely.

She nodded and took a sip. "Thank you. This is lovely. Tuck in to the food, everyone. Just help yourselves." She moved over to the table and began to load up a plate.

When they were all sitting down with their food, Sarah looked over at Adam. "What job do you do, then, Chris? Must be something lucrative, for you to be able to afford Champagne."

Olivia glanced over at him and saw his eyes glinting with mischief. She held her breath.

"Oh, I'm a serial killer," he said calmly, taking a bite of pizza. There was a moment's silence as everyone stared at him. "But it's okay. I'm on holiday this week. It's Christmas."

Olivia emitted a little squeak, and fell back against the cushions, her hand pressed against her mouth and tears of laughter filling her eyes.

"Your faces!" she managed at last. "That was priceless! A serial killer on holiday!"

Sarah rolled her eyes. "Oh, you're such a comedian," she said. "So what do you really do?"

"Computer programming. But I'm still on holiday this week."

"I thought you said he was a data entry processor or something?" Jess looked curiously at Olivia.

"I changed my job." Adam smiled at her. "That was way too boring. Not me at all."

"Okay." Jess looked unconvinced.

"I work in computers too." Tom nodded to him. "Do you work in London?"

"The company I work for is based in Bristol." Adam shrugged. "But they have an office in London too, and I split my time between them."

"Oh. However did you meet Olivia, then?" Sarah stared at him in surprise.

"He was a data entry processor when we met," Olivia cut in before Adam could dig himself in any deeper. "Then he worked all the time in London. Now he just has a flat in London and spends some time there and some time in Bristol."

"Ah, right." Jess frowned. "So what's the company you work for in Bristol?"

"Munro Solutions."

"Shit!" Tom stared at him. "They're massive. They brought out that new search engine in the summer. Boodle Search. That's taking over everywhere. Did you have anything to do with that?"

"Of course not," Olivia cut in again. "He was still data processing back then. We've only been together a few months. He changed jobs fairly recently." She stared intently at Adam, daring him to disagree.

"Yeah, that's right. It's a great system, though. I'd thoroughly recommend it." He smiled at Olivia and slipped his arm around her shoulders. "It's nice having a better job, of course. Now I can afford to treat Olivia to nice things."

"Like the Champagne." Sarah nodded, and drained her glass. "Did you say there's another bottle?"

"For tomorrow!" Olivia rolled her eyes. She moved slightly closer to Adam, and he tightened his arm around her. Her mind was spinning at his revelation that he worked for Munro Solutions. He had already told her his name was Munro, and since he clearly wasn't short of money, she had a suspicion that his family probably owned the business.

She had a lot to discuss with him when they were on their own. Maybe this was the sort of thing he should have told her. She looked up at him, and he immediately bent his head and kissed her on the lips. She closed her eyes and felt her whole body tingle, and she pressed even closer to him.

"Oh, get a room, you two!" Sarah's disgusted voice cut through, and they pulled apart, Olivia's head still spinning. Adam gave her a little smile and the hint of a wink and tightened his arm around her.

"Sorry, guys. I've been away a lot lately, so it's a

real treat to be able to spend some time with Olivia." The lies tripped off his tongue so smoothly that Olivia almost found herself believing them. She decided to make the most of the moment and snuggled even closer to him.

"Yes. We really missed each other. This is so nice to be able to spend several whole days together."

She saw Jess watching her, a speculative glint in her eye, and decided she would have to try and avoid all situations where she might be alone with her. She had always had a problem lying to her best friend and was afraid she would give it all away if she had to talk to her. That was the trouble with friends who had known you all your life. They were very difficult to fool.

"So what's the plan for tomorrow?" Tom glanced around at them all. "Are we having presents under the tree, or what?"

"Yeah, absolutely!" Sarah sat up. "I reckon we should put them all under there in a minute, and we can prod them to see what we think they are."

"No prodding allowed." Adam shook his head with mock severity. "Who brought you up? We were never allowed to prod."

"Well, neither was I as a kid." Sarah grinned. "I think now I'm nearly twenty-six I should be allowed to. Just one present."

"No," they all shouted at once, and Sarah burst out laughing.

"Okay, okay! I know when I'm beaten. I'll be patient."

"Good. We'll put them out just before we all go to bed." Jon raised an eyebrow at Sarah. "Just to lessen the temptation. Have we got any way to listen to music?"

"I brought my laptop," Olivia said. "I've got quite a lot of music on that. Shall I get it?"

"Oh, god, not the stuff you like!" Sarah rolled her eyes. "How do you cope with her dreadful musical taste, Chris? I've no idea where she gets it from."

Olivia glanced at Adam, realising he had no idea of her musical taste. She sniffed. "My taste is fine. Just because you don't like nineties stuff doesn't mean no one else does. I think that dance stuff you like is rubbish. Anyway, I have quite a selection on my laptop."

"Nineties stuff is cool." Adam glanced down at Olivia. "She has good taste. Obviously, as her taste in men demonstrates."

"Liv, how do you put up with him?" Sarah was grinning widely. "He's a bit full of himself, isn't he?"

"I can cope." Olivia snuggled even closer to Adam and smiled serenely.

"Well, go and get your laptop, then." Sarah sighed. "I guess that would be better than nothing. Anything to stop you two being so lovey dovey!"

"Sarah, that's just mean." Jon perched on the arm of her chair. "Maybe we should take a leaf out of their book? Move over." He slid down on top of her and put his arm round her neck. "There. We can be lovey dovey too."

"Get off." Sarah pushed him off her lap onto the floor. "You can wait till we go to bed. Laptop, Liv?"

With a sigh, Olivia disentangled herself from Adam's arm and ran up to the bedroom to fetch her laptop. At least if they put music on it might stop people asking Adam questions he either couldn't or shouldn't answer. She smiled to herself as she made her way back downstairs. She was beginning to really enjoy the pretence.

Chapter 4

"Night, then." Olivia waved a hand as they all disappeared into their respective bedrooms, then took a deep breath and pushed open the door to hers. Adam was standing by the window, staring out at the sea. He turned as she entered.

"This is a nice room. Lovely evening, by the way."

"Yes, it was nice. Even Sarah was bearable."

"More or less." He grinned and walked across the room towards her. "Needs watching, that one. And I wasn't sure Jess was convinced by my story."

"I don't think she was." Olivia shook her head. "I shall have to try and avoid being alone with her. She'll start asking awkward questions. It really would have been much easier if you'd agreed to say you were a data entry processor."

"I'm sorry, I just couldn't." He smiled down at her. "I don't even know what it is, and it sounds ghastly."

"And you could have told me who you really were."

"Why? It wasn't really relevant."

"It would have been nice to know I was pretending to date a millionaire who owns a computer software company."

"My dad owns it."

"Don't split hairs." She frowned at him. "I guess you're pretty important."

"I'm the MD." He shrugged. "Dad decided to semi-retire last year, and I took over. He keeps an eye on the Californian side of the business, but I basically have free rein over here."

"And Boodle Search?"

"Yeah. That was me. One of my better efforts."

"Good grief." Olivia sat down on the bed. "And you're spending Christmas in a tiny cottage with a load of strangers, pretending to be an under-achieving Londoner."

Adam burst out laughing and sat down beside her. "And having great fun. Your friends are great, and so are you. Aren't you having fun?"

"Yeah." She looked up at him. "But you could be anywhere. You could have gone on a cruise, stayed at the Ritz…"

"I could, but I wasn't going to. I was planning on spending Christmas in my own home with Naomi."

"Just the two of you?"

"Yes. And to be perfectly honest, I wasn't really looking forward to it. This is far more fun." He grinned at her. "And I've never bought clothes in a supermarket before."

Olivia giggled. "Well, I was a bit surprised when you asked if you needed a tux! Now you've met my friends, I'm sure you can see why."

"Yeah, and it's so much nicer not to have to worry about things like that. I've got so used to going to posh events and having to dress up that this is a great relief."

"Won't anyone be wondering where you are?"

"Only Naomi and my ex-best friend. I'm not due back at work until after the New Year, and as I told you, my parents and sister are scattered around the world. So long as they can reach me on my phone they won't be concerned."

"So you really like being here?"

"Yes. If I didn't, I would have gone to a hotel, like I told you. That would have been really depressing."

Olivia looked down at her hands in her lap and wondered how to broach the subject of the sleeping arrangements. Apart from the bed, there was very little furniture in the room. Just a small chest of drawers, a very old-fashioned walnut wardrobe, and the wooden chair she had wedged under the door handle the night before. The bare wooden floor had a couple of small rugs thrown on it. It certainly wasn't suitable to be slept on. She glanced down at the bed. Suppose they both slept in it? Could that work?

"Are you wondering what to do about sleeping?" Adam's voice cut into her thoughts.

She nodded. "We don't really have a lot of choice."

"I could sneak down and sleep on the sofa after the others have gone to bed, if you like?"

"No." She shook her head. "That won't work. One of them will find you somehow or other and then how could we explain it? They think we're all over each other."

"Well we did give that impression." He smiled. "I thought we did that well, actually. What do you think?"

"Very well."

"I think we could manage in the bed." He glanced at it. "It's big enough for a side each."

"Well, you can't sleep on the floor." Olivia shook her head. "In fact, you're still injured after yesterday. You really need to sleep in a proper bed."

"And it's your cottage. I can't turn you out of your

bed, so the only other option is for us to share." He looked solemnly at her. "I promise not to sleep naked."

Olivia giggled. "Bit cold for that, I think." She smiled at him. "Okay, then, I guess we'll have to. I don't trust Sarah not to barge in on us in the morning anyway. It would look a bit weird if one of us was on the floor."

"Doesn't the door lock?"

"No. As I discovered last night."

"Last night? You wanted to lock it last night?" Adam looked at her quizzically.

She felt her face get hot, and turned away. "Well, I wasn't totally sure you weren't a serial killer, at that point, and I could just hear what my mother would say if I didn't lock my door."

"But you couldn't?"

"No." She glanced round at him under her lashes. "Don't laugh, but I wedged the chair under the door handle. Just in case."

"And you thought that would stop a serial killer?" He was looking at her in amusement.

"Well, it might have. I didn't *really* think you were a serial killer. It was just a precaution."

"And you don't feel the need for that precaution tonight?"

"Well, not much I can do about it now, is there? Here you are, already in the room." She grinned at him. "If you're going to kill me, I'm sure you will anyway. I'll take the chance."

"Good. Right, let's get to bed, then. It's bloody freezing up here." Adam stood up, pulled his shirt over his head, and rummaged in one of his carrier bags.

Olivia watched him out of the corner of her eye.

Without his shirt on he was even more gorgeous than fully clothed, and she couldn't help a little shiver of anticipation when she realised she would be spending the night just a few inches away from him.

She stood up and pulled her sweater over her head. She removed her bra without taking off her T-shirt and made the decision to sleep in that one rather than change. She peeled off her socks and removed her jewellery. That done, she turned round to see how Adam was getting on.

He had changed into a white T-shirt and a pair of blue check pyjama bottoms. His discarded clothes were in a heap in the middle of the floor, but Olivia decided to ignore them, and sat down on the bed. She fished in her bag and pulled out her phone, placing it on the small bedside table.

"Shall we set an alarm?"

"Do we need to?" Adam pulled back the cover and slid into bed. "I'm sure we'll wake up fairly early."

"What time is it now?" Olivia picked up the phone again. "Oh, nearly midnight. It's nearly Christmas Day." She got to her feet and walked over to the window. The curtains were still open, and she stared out at the full moon reflecting on the shimmering sea. Her gaze slid upwards to the dark starry sky and lingered there a moment or two.

"What are you looking at?" Adam had got out of bed and joined her at the window.

"Nothing. Just the moon." She kept her face turned away from him.

"When I was little, I always used to look up into the sky before I went to bed on Christmas Eve. Just in case." He spoke quietly and leaned forward to peer through the glass.

"Do you still do it?" Olivia's voice was little more than a whisper.

"Sometimes. It adds to the magic."

"It does." She stared up into the sky. "My mother does it. I always thought we were odd, but you understand. I just have to look, just before I go to bed. Silly, isn't it?"

"No. Not silly at all." He slipped his arm around her shoulders. "It means you're still in touch with your childhood. You've not been spoiled by age."

"Maybe lots of people do it." Olivia turned away from the window and shivered. "But I've never met anyone else who admitted to it."

His arm still around her shoulders, Adam steered her towards the bed. "Get in, you're freezing."

She walked round to the other side of the bed and slid in under the quilt. He was right; she was very cold, and the chilly clean sheets did nothing to help that. She lay on her back and pulled the quilt up to her chin. Adam had got in beside her, and he was close enough for her to feel the warmth from his body. His gorgeous, very sexy body. That was less than six inches away from her.

"I'm cold too." He reached over and touched her arm with his hand. "You know, if we moved a bit closer, we could keep each other warm."

"I suppose it would be silly for us to stay cold if there was something we could do about it." Olivia didn't move.

"Well, it would, really," Adam agreed. "If we froze to death and your friends found us in the morning, they'd never understand how it happened. We have to keep up the pretence."

"I suppose we do. Just to keep warm, then."

"Of course. Just to keep warm. Might be a nice way to get to know each other better, too."

Olivia rolled onto her side and stared at him. "How well?"

"Just well enough." Adam rolled to face her. "We can talk while we warm each other up. Less chance of getting caught out by suspicious friends then."

"Okay." Olivia gave a little smile. "I guess that would be all right. But we keep our pyjamas on."

"Of course! We hardly know each other." Adam grinned at her. "Come on, then, meet you in the middle."

They both wriggled into the centre of the bed until their bodies were just touching.

"Hello."

Olivia could feel his breath on her face. "Hello."

"You have lovely eyes."

"They're just wishy-washy blue."

"They're beautiful. Don't put yourself down." He reached up and hooked a strand of hair behind her ear. "Lovely hair, too."

"Now you're just being silly." Olivia wriggled. "My hair is boring mousey brown, and just straight."

"You don't take compliments very well, do you?" His voice was amused. "Relax. Come a bit closer. You're still cold." He put his arms around her and pulled her closer to him. "That's better. I'm not going to murder you, you know. Or ravish you. Just keep you warm."

Olivia let herself relax against him, the feel of his warmth sending shock waves through her body. What on earth was going on? How did she end up here? In bed with a beautiful man who only yesterday she had found unconscious on the beach. A man she still knew very little about and who was only there because he was doing her a favour because he thought he owed it to her.

She moved her head slightly and looked up at him. But if he really was only there through a sense of duty, why had he been complimenting her and why did she have the overwhelming feeling he was about to kiss her again? The kisses in front of her friends had been for a reason. They had been lovely, but she was under no illusion that they were for anything other than show. Yet now…

His lips were less than an inch away from her own, and as she raised her head, their eyes locked.

"I think I may be about to kiss you again," Adam murmured softly, his lips almost touching her own. "Just for practice for tomorrow, you understand."

"Of course," Olivia whispered, her body quivering with anticipation. "We need the practice."

Very gently he pressed his lips onto hers, and his arms tightened around her. Olivia's head began to spin, and she closed her eyes and pressed her body hard against him. Sliding her arms around him, she parted her lips as his tongue slipped out and gently probed her mouth.

Urgently their tongues entwined, their bodies pressing ever closer together, Olivia feeling she was about to explode with desire. His hands moved over her body, gently caressing her breasts through her thin T-shirt, until he pulled back slightly and smiled down at her.

"I think we maybe ought to stop there." His eyes

were clouded with passion. "Otherwise we may not be able to stop at all."

Olivia's arms were still around his body. Her mind was screaming at him to carry on, but she heard her voice agreeing with him. "I suppose so. But that was very nice."

"Very nice?" Adam pulled back a bit more and looked down at her. "Very nice? Is that the best you can do?" He laughed and rolled onto his back. "We're getting quite good at this kissing lark. Maybe practise a bit more in the morning?"

"Before we get up?"

"Before we get up."

"I'll set an alarm, then." Olivia leaned over and fiddled with her phone. "I would hate to think we woke too late to do it."

She lay down again and turned to face him. "You have lovely eyes too. I've never seen such green eyes before."

"Thank you. You see, that's how you should accept a compliment." He grinned at her and slid his arm around her. "Now cuddle up and let's get some sleep. We have a busy day playacting tomorrow, and you need all the rest you can get. Oh, and Happy Christmas."

"Happy Christmas." Olivia smiled to herself as she rested her head on his shoulder and closed her eyes.

Chapter 5

Christmas Day

"Good morning. Merry Christmas."

Olivia opened her eyes and found Adam lying on his side watching her. "Merry Christmas. Did the alarm go off? I didn't hear it."

"No, not yet. But I was awake, so I thought you should be too. More time to practise the kissing."

Olivia smiled at him and yawned. "Mmm. Nice idea. Need to be able to make it convincing."

Adam put out an arm and pulled her towards him. She wriggled closer and pressed her body against his. "You're much warmer this morning." He smiled at her. "That's good." He bent his head, and his warm lips locked onto hers, causing her heart to leap in her chest.

She snaked her arms around his neck and wound her fingers into his hair, pressing her body more firmly against his. Gently his tongue parted her lips, and Olivia thought she was actually going to die from pleasure as their tongues entwined and his fingers flicked lightly across her erect nipples, still covered by the thin T-shirt.

"Are you two awake?" The voice was accompanied by a loud banging on the bedroom door, and they pulled apart reluctantly.

"No." Adam rolled his eyes and dropped a light

kiss on the end of Olivia's nose. "We're still fast asleep. Go away."

The door opened and Sarah's head appeared, her long blonde hair tousled by sleep. "Come on, put each other down, it's time for presents. Jon has put the kettle on."

"Are Jess and Tom up?" Olivia rolled onto her back and kept the cover pulled up to her chin.

"We've woken them. Now come on down or I'll start prodding the presents." She vanished, leaving the door to slam shut behind her, and Olivia looked over at Adam.

"We'd better do as she says. She can be a bit like a spoilt child if she doesn't get her own way."

"Yes. I can tell." Adam grinned. "Oh, well, never mind. I think we can keep them fooled today with a few well-timed kisses. What do you say?"

"Absolutely. I'm sure we can." They stared at each other for a moment, and Olivia was slightly unnerved by a fleeting expression in Adam's eyes. She looked away and swung her legs out of bed. What had that been?

She was beginning to think he might possibly have feelings for her other than just the need to repay a debt, but she couldn't be sure. Although the kissing last night that had nearly led to something else had certainly indicated that. She stood up and peered into the small mirror on the wall.

"I guess we'd better get downstairs, then. I'll just try and do something about my hair first, though. Looks like a haystack."

"It looks fine. Leave it. It'll add to our story."

Olivia glanced over her shoulder at him. "What

d'you mean?"

"Trust me. Just leave it." Adam rolled out of bed and stretched. "So we're opening presents in our pyjamas, are we?"

"Oh, yeah. No way Sarah will wait for us to get dressed. Come on, we can have a coffee to wake us up." She glanced in the mirror again. "I still think I should sort my hair, though…"

"Nope. Leave it." Adam put his hand on her back and gave her a gentle push towards the door. "Off you go. Let's keep your friends happy."

Jess and Tom appeared out of their room at the same time, and the four of them made their way down the stairs exchanging Christmas wishes.

"Did you sleep okay?" Olivia asked.

"Not bad. It was a bit cold." Jess shivered and pulled her dressing gown around her. "Took a while to get off to sleep."

"Our room was cold, too." Adam looked over his shoulder at her. "We found a way to keep warm, though."

Olivia felt Jess's eyes on her and hastened down the stairs. Now was not the time to face any questions.

Sarah was kneeling on the floor in front of the small tree, peering closely at the piled-up presents, obviously desperately trying not to touch them. Olivia laughed.

"Honestly, Sarah, you're like a six-year-old. We're all here now. Let's just get some coffee, and then we can get stuck in."

"Coffee's made." Jon's voice wafted out from the kitchen. "Come and help yourselves to milk and sugar. I put the mince pies out too, in case anyone fancies one."

"Awesome." Olivia dived into the kitchen and poured milk into her coffee. "This is great. Thanks, Jon." She carried her mug out into the living room and curled up in the corner of the sofa. Adam was squatting down in front of the woodburner. "Is it still lit?"

"Just." He picked up some sticks and placed them carefully on the fire. "These should get it going, and then I'll add a log in a minute."

"You're so clever." Sarah was watching him with admiration. "I'd have no idea how one of those things worked."

"You townies." He laughed at her. "Olivia was the same when we first arrived. No idea how to light a fire."

"You're a townie too, though, aren't you, Chris?" Jess curled herself into a chair, her keen eyes fixed on him. "How come you know so much about it?"

"I live in a town now." He put the log on the fire and closed it up. "But when I was younger we spent a lot of time at my grandparents' house. It's very old and has several open fires." He stood up and smiled at Jess. "Even people in towns have fires too, you know."

Sarah shuffled over and warmed her hands in front of the stove. "Come on, guys, dying to get at these pressies! Hurry up."

"Hope you've got some presents worth having." Olivia grinned at her. "You're really building this up."

"Oh, all presents are worth having." Sarah tossed her head. "And you can stop looking so smug with your just-fucked hair. We all know what you two did to keep warm last night."

Olivia felt her face begin to get hot and raised her

coffee to her lips. "I don't know what you mean," she muttered, carefully avoiding catching Adam's eye. Now she realised what he'd meant about her hair. She wondered if they might be taking the playacting too far.

She looked up and caught Jess watching her, and her heart sank. She recognised that look. It wouldn't be long before her best friend cornered her and started asking awkward questions.

"Okay, everyone ready?" Sarah looked round at them all. "Let's start. Shall I hand them out?"

"Go on, then." Jon grinned at her. "We won't keep you waiting any longer."

With an excited squeak, Sarah moved over to the tree and picked up the first present. "This is for…Jess." She handed the present over and pulled out the next one.

When they each had a small pile of presents in front of them, Sarah moved over to sit next to Jon, and smiled. "Okay, you may open them now!"

Olivia looked down at her own pile of presents and wondered which was the one from Adam. She picked up the first one, beautifully wrapped in metallic paper and decorated with ribbon.

"That's from me and Jon," Sarah called across the room. "Isn't the paper nice?"

"Lovely." Olivia smiled and unpeeled the sticky tape carefully. "It seems a shame to rip it." The present proved to be a box of very expensive chocolates, and she blew a kiss across the room. "Thank you, Sarah. You know me so well."

"Pleasure, darling. And thank you for yours." Sarah was surrounded by a pile of torn paper and was already painting her nails with the blue metallic polish

Olivia had given her.

"Our pleasure." Olivia picked up her next present. It was almost square and mostly soft, with a small hard lump in the middle. She peered at the card. It was from Adam. She glanced at him as she started to peel off the tape.

"I hope I chose well." He was watching her, a small smile playing around his lips. "Not used to buying Christmas presents in a supermarket. The choice was limited."

"I'm sure it'll be fine." She ripped the paper and stared down at the contents, her face beginning to flame. He had bought her underwear. She slowly unfolded the silky pants and camisole top, her hands shaking. He had bought her underwear. He had even got the size right.

"Wow, that's pretty." Jess looked up in surprise. "Is that from Chris?"

Olivia nodded, totally unable to speak. She felt under the clothes and located the hard object. It was a small bottle of perfume.

"I thought it smelled nice." Adam shrugged. "Hope you do too. And I think I got your size right."

She nodded silently, still unable to form any words. He had bought her underwear. She had known him for less than two days, and he had bought her underwear. She took the top off the perfume and applied a little to her wrist. He was right; it smelled lovely. Taking a deep breath, she turned to him and forced her mouth into a smile.

"Thank you. It's lovely. And yes, you got the size right."

"Good. I think you'll look nice in those. Now,

which one is from you?" Silently she pointed to her carefully wrapped parcel. He picked it up and smiled at her. "Hmmm. Looks like a book, I think." He ripped off the paper and stared down at the volume in his hand, his face almost immediately breaking into a huge grin.

"I thought it might amuse you." Olivia finally found her voice.

"It does." He leaned over and kissed her on the lips. "It really does. Thank you."

"What is it?" Having unwrapped all her presents, Sarah was watching the others. "What has she given you?"

"*Serial Killers Unmasked.*" Adam held the book up for them all to see.

"Oh, right." Sarah frowned. "Because you said you were a serial killer? You two have a weird sense of humour."

Olivia finished unwrapping her presents, then got to her feet. "Anyone want more tea or coffee?" They all did, so she gathered up the mugs. "Come and give me a hand, Chris." Adam followed her to the kitchen, and she drew him into the corner. "You bought me underwear?" she whispered. "I bought you a silly book about serial killers and you bought me sexy underwear and perfume. What on earth will the others think?"

"That I'm a thoughtful boyfriend?" He grinned at her. "Why are you so worried? Isn't that the sort of thing a boyfriend of three months might give you? I thought it was. We have to make this believable, remember."

Olivia turned away from him and refilled the kettle. He had only bought the underwear and perfume to make it look believable. Not because he thought she'd like them. "Okay. I guess you're right."

"And I thought you'd look nice in them, too."

She looked over her shoulder at him to see if he was being serious. "What's that supposed to mean?"

"Just what I said. I wanted to get you something suitable for the pretence, but also something I thought you'd like. And I really like that perfume."

She turned away again and got the jar of coffee out of the cupboard. So he *had* bought them because he thought she'd like them. This was all getting too complicated. She spooned the coffee into the mugs and turned back to face him again.

"Okay. Thank you. I bought the book because I thought it would make you laugh. But maybe it was the wrong thing to buy a boyfriend."

"Not at all." He moved a bit closer to her. "You rightly determined that I have a good sense of humour, not dissimilar to your own, I think, and got me the perfect present. Thank you."

"Well, if you say so." She looked up at him. "But underwear? You hardly know me."

"I'm getting to know you better all the time." He moved even closer and put his hands on her shoulders. "I really think we need to have another practice with the kissing. We got interrupted this morning."

"What, now?"

"Yes, now." His lips came down on hers, and he slid his arms around her, pulling her closer. Olivia felt herself begin to go lightheaded and put her hands on his shoulders. He gently parted her lips, and they clung together, their tongues both urgently probing. Olivia pressed her body closer to his and felt his hands begin to caress her waist and move down to cup her buttocks.

"Can I have a word?"

Jess's voice shocked them both back to reality, and they pulled apart slowly. Olivia looked over Adam's shoulder. "Right now?"

"Right now."

Adam let go of Olivia and turned round. "Shall I leave?"

"No, this concerns you too." Jess closed the kitchen door and leant against the work surface. "There's something odd going on here, and I want to know what it is."

"What d'you mean?" Olivia shuffled her feet uncomfortably. "We were just kissing. People do that."

"Yes, people do. Boyfriends and girlfriends do." Jess was watching them both with narrowed eyes. "The thing is, I'm just not totally convinced that you two *are* boyfriend and girlfriend."

"Don't be daft." Olivia took hold of Adam's hand. "Of course we are, what are you talking about?"

"This man doesn't look anything like the Chris you described to me. There is no way you wouldn't have told me if he was this good-looking."

Adam smirked, and Olivia squeezed his hand. "I really don't know what you mean, Jess. Of course this is Chris. You probably weren't listening properly when I told you about him. Did you see this necklace my mum gave me, by the way?"

"Liv, I'm not Sarah. I can't be distracted by shiny objects or alcohol. I don't believe this is Chris, and I want to know what you're up to."

"Where's that coffee?" The door swung open and Sarah's head appeared. "You've been ages."

"Sorry, just coming." Olivia turned to the kettle

and flicked it back on again. "If you hang on, you can take a couple with you." She poured the hot water into the mugs, uncomfortably aware of Jess's eyes on her back. "Here you go. You take these, and Jess, you take these. Chris and I will bring ours." She held out the mugs to the two girls and watched as they walked through into the living room, Jess casting a suspicious glance at them as she disappeared.

"Oh, god. What do we do now?" Olivia stared up at Adam. "She won't let it go. She'll follow us around until we tell her."

"Well, we'll just have to make it even more obvious that we *are* boyfriend and girlfriend, then." Adam slipped his arm around her shoulders and gave her a squeeze. "I don't think that will be too much of a hardship. Will it?"

Olivia managed a small smile. "I guess I'll cope. But please don't be fooled into thinking Jess will forget about this. I know her." She picked up her mug and walked back into the living room.

"So what are we going to do today, then?" Tom raised his eyebrows. "Apart from eat and drink, of course."

"That'll probably take up most of the day." Sarah grinned. "I hope so, anyway. I wonder what film is on this afternoon?"

"Oh, god, not the Christmas Day movie!" Olivia groaned. "It'll be some kids' cartoon probably. Do we have to?"

"We could play games again," Adam suggested, sitting down on the sofa and pulling Olivia down next to him. "That was fun, playing Cluedo yesterday."

"We have Cluedo?" Tom's eyes lit up. "I love

Cluedo."

"Yeah, we played it while we were waiting for you two to arrive." Sarah yawned. "I'm really bad at it. We could play one of the other games. But not Monopoly. That always causes fights in our house."

Olivia glanced round at them all. "Well, firstly, I think we should all get dressed. No slobbing around in pjs today. In fact, it might be fun to dress up a bit. You know, look really smart. We have Champagne to have with lunch, so let's dress accordingly."

Sarah laughed. "Okay. Could be fun. I brought loads of clothes."

"All right." Jess shrugged. "I brought a nice dress. Why not?" She sounded a bit subdued, and Olivia glanced at her nervously. She was sure they hadn't heard the last of Jess's suspicions, and she just hoped she didn't bring the subject up in front of the others. That could get really embarrassing. If they had to end up confessing to Jess, then so be it, but she really didn't want the others to know.

Adam drained his mug and stood up. "That's a good idea. Come on, let's go and get dressed." He held out his hand and pulled Olivia to her feet. "You can wear your Christmas present."

"Don't you think I'd be more suitably attired in a dress?"

"If you must." He grinned down at her. "But at least I'll know you're well dressed underneath."

"Are you casting aspersions on my taste in dresses?" She followed him up the stairs, aware of Jess's eyes still on them.

"I'll let you know." They had reached the bedroom, and Adam opened the door and stood aside for her to go through.

"Thank you. You have lovely manners."

"I was well brought up." He walked over to the window and stared out at the churning sea. "It's really wild out there today. Might be fun to go for a walk later."

Olivia joined him. "It looks very cold. But if we wrapped up it might be fun. You'd have to promise to keep off the rocks, though."

"Are you worried about me?" He glanced down at her with a smile.

"Yes. If you fell again, you might not be so lucky next time."

"In what way was I lucky? Being rescued by a beautiful girl and carried off to her lair?"

"No, you idiot. You were lucky not to get concussion, or do more damage."

"Ah, right." He grinned at her. "But I'd still get rescued and kidnapped by the beautiful girl, would I?"

"You might." Olivia raised an eyebrow. "But you might not be in a fit state to appreciate it. Now, come on, let's get dressed."

"I like your plan of getting dressed up. Was that because of the tux?"

"Partly." She smiled at him as she delved into her bag and pulled out some clothes. "But I suddenly thought it would be fun. I haven't been out much lately and really wanted to get dressed up nice."

"So what was a typical date for you and Chris, then?" Adam was emptying out his plastic bags onto the bed.

"Oh, an evening down the pub with his mates. Talking about football." She grimaced. "Certainly no need to wear anything other than jeans."

"I honestly can't imagine you doing that." Adam was watching her curiously as he slipped his arms into a crisp white shirt. "I don't think you were very well suited."

"We weren't." Olivia sighed and held a blue silky dress up against her. "But he asked me out, and I hadn't had a date in months, so I said yes. It just sort of carried on from there."

"Well, thank goodness it's over now."

Olivia looked over at him. "Why?"

"He wasn't right for you, or good enough for you." He pulled on a pair of very dark grey trousers and zipped them up. "That dress is nice. Are you going to wear it?"

"I think so." She laid it on the bed and studied it. "I only brought two, but I think this is the nicest. You're looking smart." And very hot, she added in her head, watching as he produced a tie from the pile of clothes on the bed. "I didn't know supermarkets sold ties."

"I was amazed by what I managed to get." Adam grinned at her and expertly fastened the tie. "I even managed to get a waistcoat to go with the suit."

"You bought a whole suit?" Olivia stared at him in surprise.

"I told you I bought something to cover every possible social occasion. Almost."

"You look very nice." She stepped into her dress and twisted round to do up the zip.

"Thank you. Let me help you with that." He moved across the room and, putting one hand on her shoulder, he gently eased the zip up the back of her dress. "There. Is that okay?"

"Thank you." She stood very still, savouring the feel of his hands on her body. He seemed in no hurry to move them, and she glanced over her shoulder at him.

"We still have some practising to do."

She turned around to face him. "Yes. We keep getting disturbed."

"Pity we can't lock the door. I'm not sure I trust Jess or Sarah not to burst in again."

"Use the chair." Olivia darted across the room and picked up the wooden chair. She wedged it under the door handle and grinned up at Adam. "There. That's what I did the night before last. To stop you from murdering me."

"Clever. Not sure it would deter a diligent serial killer, but it might keep us from being disturbed by your friends." He pulled her towards him. "Now, where were we?"

"Something like this, I think." Olivia put her hands on his shoulders and stood on tiptoe until she could reach his lips. He put his arms around her and pulled her closer, his lips meeting hers and his hands caressing her body. Olivia felt her legs turn to jelly as his tongue entered her mouth, and her whole body started to tingle with desire.

"Are you ready, you two?" Sarah's voice was accompanied by a tap on the door, followed by the handle being rattled. "Have you locked the door? God! Are you having sex? Now?"

With a sigh, Adam pulled away from Olivia. "No, we're getting dressed. In private. We didn't want an audience. We'll be there in a minute." He looked down at her with a wry grin. "We don't seem destined to finish this kiss, do we? All the more reason to go for a little walk later."

"You think we still need more practice, then?" Olivia was trying to smooth her hair.

"Definitely. You can't practise something like this too much. We really need to be believable."

"Of course. We need to be believable." She turned away and hooked some earrings into her ears. "We must keep fooling the others."

"Well, I think Sarah is pretty convinced." Adam was buttoning up his waistcoat. "That's the second time she's thought we were having sex."

"Yes." Olivia finished putting her jewellery on and slipped her feet into a pair of very high black court shoes.

"You look amazing."

She looked up to find Adam watching her, a strange expression on his face. She felt herself blush and looked down at her nails. "Thank you. You look pretty good yourself."

He walked round the bed to join her and stopped directly in front of her. "In fact, you look more than amazing. You look completely gorgeous." He bent forward and placed a light kiss on her lips, then unhooked the chair from under the door handle and held out his arm. "Shall we?"

Silently she took it, and together they left the room and walked down the stairs to the living room. The other four were already there, and they all looked up as Olivia and Adam made their way down.

"Wow!" Sarah stared at them. "You two look fantastic! I thought you were gorgeous before, Chris, but now…"

Jon slapped her arm. "Behave yourself, woman.

Liv, you look great. Didn't realise you scrubbed up that well."

"Thank you, I think." Olivia grinned as they reached the bottom of the stairs. "You all look great too. It's fun to dress up sometimes. I certainly don't get to often enough."

"You not taking her to posh places, then, Chris?" Jess was watching them.

"I do when I can." Adam smiled at her and put his arm around Olivia's shoulders. "But like I said, I've been away so much recently we haven't really had much chance. I'm hoping all that's going to change after the New Year." His arm tightened around her, and he dropped a light kiss on the top of her head.

Olivia slipped her arm around his waist and smiled serenely at Jess. "I'm looking forward to that. He's got some great things planned."

"Ooh, what?" Sarah stared at them with wide eyes. "Is he taking you up to London?"

"I live in London, Sarah."

"You know what I mean, up West. To a show, or out for dinner or something."

"Tell her, Chris. Where are you taking me?" She looked up at him, mischief in her eyes.

Adam held her gaze, his face inscrutable, while he spoke. "Well, to start with, I thought afternoon tea at the Ritz would be nice. They really spoil you there. Followed by a trip to the theatre, and ending up dancing at a very select club I know." He raised his eyebrows. "How does that sound, Olivia?"

"Perfect, thank you, Chris." She found she couldn't tear her eyes away from his and had to fight an overwhelming desire to pull him down onto the sofa and completely devour him. "That would be a lovely day."

"That would cost a fortune." Sarah was staring at them, almost drooling with envy.

"She's worth it." Adam unwound his arm from Olivia's shoulders and walked over to tend to the fire. "I think we might make it a weekend, actually."

"Munro Solutions must pay very well." Jess perched on the arm of the sofa and watched him as he loaded logs onto the fire. "Tom doesn't earn nearly enough for that sort of trip, and he works in computers."

"I'm not a programmer, Jess." Tom shook his head. "Top programmers get a lot more than me."

"But you were a data processor or whatever, until recently." Jess was persistent. "How can you now be a top programmer?"

"Jess, that's a bit rude." Olivia frowned at her. "Is it really any of your business?"

"Just curious." Jess held her gaze. "It's not a secret, is it?"

Adam closed the fire and stood up. "I was a programmer first, Jess. I was only doing the data processing because I needed a job in a hurry. I've programmed before, so when I joined Munro I went in at quite a good salary." He smiled at her. "They're very generous payers, actually."

Olivia turned away, unable to prevent herself from grinning, and walked into the kitchen. "What time is lunch? I see the turkey's in."

"About one." Jon followed her. "You can do the veg if you like. I daren't let Sarah anywhere near them. She can even mess up a boiled egg."

Olivia opened a cupboard and pulled out a couple of large saucepans. "No problem. I quite like doing veggies. I brought potatoes, carrots, and sprouts. Did anyone else bring any?"

"There's some sweet corn in a tin, but other than that, no." Jon grinned at her. "I'll leave you to it, and I'll be back to baste the turkey in a while. Can we use your laptop for music again?"

"Of course." Olivia pushed her hair out of her eyes. "Can you ask Chris to come in? He can peel the spuds."

She was just preparing the sprouts when Adam came up behind her. He put his hands on her waist and leaned his chin on her head. "Need some help?"

"Not really. Just wanted to talk to you."

"Okay." He gently turned her around to face him. "Would you like some more practice?"

She looked up at him solemnly. "Do you think you're taking this playacting rather too far?"

"What do you mean?"

"Tea at the Ritz, the theatre, and dancing in a club? Bit over the top."

"Why? That's exactly the sort of date I'd take you on."

"But we're not really going out."

"They think we are." He looked down at her. "Stop worrying about it. And I managed to explain the whole programmer thing, too."

"She didn't believe you." Olivia gently ran her finger along the blade of the knife she was holding. "She'll probably appear in a minute and start asking questions again."

Adam took the knife out of her hand and placed it on the chopping board. "Let's not play with sharp objects. Now, come here. We still need more practice." He pulled her into his arms and pressed his lips gently against hers.

Unable to resist, Olivia melted against him, returning the kiss and parting her lips when his tongue began to probe. She slipped her arms around his neck and pressed even closer, loving the feel of his hard body against hers.

"Oh, god, they're at it again!" Sarah appeared beside them, wine glass in hand. "There are other people here, you know. We're not all as loved up as you two. Now, where's that Champagne?"

Reluctantly pulling away from Adam, Olivia rolled her eyes. "Not yet. The Champagne's for lunch. There's some ordinary wine in the fridge. Make do with that. And poor Jon! Anyone'd think you two never even kissed these days."

"Liv, we've been going out for six years now." Sarah was rummaging in the fridge. "The first flush of excitement has worn off. Of course we kiss and have sex and all that, but not in public." She turned round, bottle in hand, and surveyed them severely. "That sort of behaviour soon stops. I'm quite surprised you're still doing it after three months, actually."

"That's very sad, Sarah." Adam put his arm round Olivia again. "It doesn't have to wear off. You can make the magic last forever, if you want." He bent over and placed a quick kiss on Olivia's lips, then winked at her and went back into the living room.

"God, he's gorgeous!" Sarah was watching him as he walked away. "Wherever did you find him?"

"You wouldn't believe me if I told you," Olivia muttered, picking up a carrot and peeling it. "Pour me a wine, will you, Sarah?"

"I finished the bottle. Shall I open another one, or do you want to wait for the Champers?"

"I'll wait." Olivia carried on peeling, her mind going over Adam's words. If only he was her real boyfriend, she would be the luckiest girl in the world. He certainly was entering into the make-believe with amazing enthusiasm, even going so far as to invent the perfect date.

"Hurry up with those veggies, Liv." Sarah peered over her shoulder. "We want to play a game."

"What game?"

"Well, Jon suggested Postman's Knock, and I must say I quite fancy it, but the others weren't so keen."

"Good. We're not twelve. I'd vote for Cluedo again." Olivia dumped the carrots into a pan and filled it up with water. "Tell them I'm just coming."

Sarah disappeared again, and Olivia tidied up the peelings, dropped them in the bin, and left the vegetables to cook on a low heat. She set the timer for fifteen minutes, wiped her hands on a tea towel, and went back into the living room.

Adam was sitting on the sofa, leaning back with his long legs stretched out in front of him, regaling the others with some tale. Sarah was hanging on his every word, sitting so close that her knee kept bumping into his. Olivia watched in amusement as he moved it slightly every time Sarah touched him, and after a minute or two had shifted significantly along the sofa. Grinning, she went to join them, sitting down at his feet and leaning her head against his knee.

"What are you all talking about?"

"Chris was telling us about the time he got stuck in

the lift in the Eiffel Tower." Tom grinned. "He had to be rescued by a fireman."

Olivia looked up over her shoulder at Adam. "You have led an exciting life," she commented, raising her eyebrows. "What other little gems haven't you told me about?"

"Hundreds, my darling, hundreds." He grinned down at her and stroked her hair. "I'll tell you some of the more interesting ones later."

Tingling from the touch of his hand on her head, and her ears ringing from hearing him call her "my darling," Olivia looked down and pretended to be picking at a nail. She never knew what was coming next with him. His idea of a walk later might be a good idea. She really needed to talk to him about just what he was saying to the others. He was in danger of going too far and getting found out. It would give them a chance to finish that practice kiss that kept getting interrupted, too.

Adam had moved his hand off her hair and was gently stroking the back of her neck with his thumb. It was sending shivers of pleasure all up and down her spine, and she had to concentrate really hard not to wriggle.

She was just thinking how he really was going all out to cement their relationship in the eyes of her friends, when glancing around she suddenly realised none of the others could see what he was doing. He was doing it solely to pleasure her. She leaned back a little further, and his fingers rubbed lightly around the base of her neck. Her skin broke out in goosebumps, and her stomach did a series of flips.

She sneaked a glance over her shoulder and caught

his eye. He winked at her and rubbed more vigorously on one point of her neck. Only just managing to hold in a squeal of pleasure, she moved forward and coughed.

"You okay, Liv?" Jess was watching her again.

"Fine." She coughed again. "Fine, thank you. Sarah said we were going to play a game."

"We were, but we couldn't agree on one." Jess sighed. "Jon wanted Postman's Knock. No takers there, obviously. I suggested Monopoly, but Sarah thinks that'll cause World War Three, and Tom wants to listen to music. What would you like, Chris?"

"Truth or Dare."

"You have *got* to be kidding!" Olivia turned round and stared at him. "Firstly, we're not sixteen, and secondly… Well, just no!"

"That could be fun." Sarah had perked up.

"No, definitely not! What's wrong with Cluedo?"

"Boring. We played that yesterday. Come on, Liv, it'll be fun."

"I was only joking." Adam put his hand on Olivia's neck again and began to rub gently. "Cluedo's fine with me."

"Me too." Tom nodded enthusiastically. "You okay with that, Jess?"

"Fine. Where is it, Livvy?"

"I'll fetch it." Olivia got to her feet just before her arousal level reached the danger zone, and shot over to the understairs cupboard. She pulled out the box and carried it over to the coffee table.

As she laid it down, her eyes locked with Adam's, and he raised his eyebrows, his eyes twinkling with mischief.

She looked away and squatted down to lay out the

board. "Here we go. This should keep us going until lunch time. Who wants to be who?"

Chapter 6

Olivia opened the back door as quietly as she could, and she and Adam slipped out into the garden. She closed it behind them, and they grinned at each other.

"Made it." Adam caught her hand. "I was beginning to think we wouldn't be able to manage to get away."

"If Jess hadn't gone upstairs, I don't think we would." Olivia opened the gate, and they stepped out onto the road. "It helped no end that Jon and Tom both went to sleep and Sarah is so busy texting she wouldn't notice if a bomb dropped in the garden. Jess was the only problem." She breathed deeply. "This is nice."

"And we can finally finish that practice kiss." Adam squeezed her hand and hurried her towards the beach. Olivia had exchanged her high heels for wellies, and they had both put on thick coats to protect against the strong wind that was blowing in off the sea. "And walk off some of that enormous lunch."

"Nice, wasn't it? I haven't eaten that much for months, though."

"And I suspect there'll be lots more food later."

"We'll probably just eat cold stuff tonight. And lots of chocolate." She smiled up at him. "Are you actually enjoying yourself? Do you like my friends?"

"Of course." He glanced down at her. "I'm

thoroughly enjoying myself. Your friends seem nice. Well, most of them, anyway."

"Sarah?"

"Yeah. She's okay, I suppose, but really annoying. The guys are nice, and Jess is okay but she unnerves me slightly."

"Because you think she's rumbled us?"

"Well, you seem to think she has." He looked at her again. "What do we do if she asks us again? Should we tell her?"

"We may have to." Olivia sighed as they left the road and started off down the beach. "I'm pretty sure she won't let it go." She let go of Adam's hand and started walking a little faster towards the sea.

"Wait up. Are you trying to get away from me?"

"No." She stopped and stared out across the churning water. "I think you should be very careful how much more you say to them all. They already think it's weird how much money you have. Remember you *are* supposed to be a boy from the east end of London who has a boring job."

"I changed his job."

"Yeah, and that's causing problems of its own." She stopped suddenly and looked round. "By the way, what the hell was that you were doing to my neck?"

Adam laughed. "I thought you were enjoying that."

"Enjoying it? I nearly had an orgasm! What were you doing?"

"I think we may have found one of your erogenous zones." He moved closer and hooked a strand of hair behind her ear. "We maybe should pursue that further, later."

"And would that be practising too?"

"I'm a great believer in practising everything until you perfect it." He had moved so close she could feel his breath on her face. "And we really ought to keep trying with that kiss. There's no one here to disturb us this time."

Olivia looked up at him seriously. "Are you enjoying this?"

"I said I was."

"No, the practising."

"Of course." He frowned down at her. "Why? Aren't you? You seem to be."

"Yes." She turned away and looked out to sea again. "I just don't like…"

"What? Olivia, what's wrong?" Adam gently turned her round to face him. "What don't you like? If it's bothering you, we could just tell them the truth."

"Can't do that." Olivia shook her head. "Then they'd have been right about me."

"What d'you mean?"

"That I'm a loser who can't keep a boyfriend."

"They wouldn't think that." Adam put his hands on her shoulders.

"They would. You heard what Sarah said when they arrived. That's why all this started."

"In that case, we must keep up the pretence." He smiled down at her. "And that will involve a lot of practising." He looked serious for a moment. "But believe me, you're definitely not a loser who can't keep a boyfriend. Don't ever think that again."

She looked up at him, and their eyes locked for a moment, causing her stomach to do a flip. He pulled her closer, and as their lips met she felt her head was going to explode.

She pressed closer and slid her arms around him, surrendering completely to the ecstasy of the kiss. Adam slipped one hand behind her head, and as his tongue gently probed her mouth, Olivia felt him start to rub the back of her neck. Almost immediately she experienced shivers of pleasure running all down her spine and she pressed closer to him, her tongue urgently entwining with his.

"Have you got a minute?"

Shocked back to reality, they pulled slightly apart and stared at Jess, clutching her coat around her against the strong breeze, her dark curls blowing across her face.

"What the fuck..." Adam muttered under his breath and gripped Olivia's hand tightly. "What d'you want, Jess?"

"We still need to talk." She walked round so her back was to the wind. "Sorry to disturb you."

"Again," Olivia managed, her body still vibrating with anticipation. "Can't it wait?"

"No. I'm sorry. It's almost impossible to get you two alone in the cottage, so I thought I'd follow you. As I said in the kitchen, something's not right here and I want to know what's going on." She wrapped her arms around herself and stamped her feet to keep warm. "There is no way this is the person you've been dating for the last three months, Liv. From what you'd said, he only ever took you to the pub and talked about football. He wouldn't even know where the Ritz was."

Olivia glanced up at Adam, and he shrugged. "Maybe have to tell her. Will she keep it quiet?"

"I hope so." Olivia sighed and fixed Jess with a stern gaze. "Okay, if you promise not to tell the others, and that includes Tom, we'll tell you the whole story."

"I knew something was up." Jess stared at them.

"This isn't Chris. You're quite right. This is Adam. I broke up with Chris, and when Sarah and Jon arrived, they assumed Adam was Chris."

"Sarah was rather rude, actually," Adam cut in. "She had had a bet with Jon that Olivia had invented Chris and that he wouldn't be here. So since she already thought I was him, I carried on the pretence."

Jess was looking confused. "Okay. So you broke up with Chris, but why didn't you just say you'd brought Adam instead and he was your new boyfriend? Wouldn't that have been easier? Why complicate things?"

"Well, it's not quite like that." Olivia was beginning to feel very awkward. "I didn't bring Adam, and we're not going out."

"You didn't bring him? So where did you get him from?" Jess looked at them in surprise.

"I found him."

"You found him?"

"Yes."

"Where?"

"Here, on the beach. Unconscious."

Jess stared at them. "You found him on the beach unconscious? What the hell…?"

"Hence the bump on my head." Adam pointed helpfully to his forehead.

"So let me get this straight." Jess closed her eyes for a moment. "You broke up with Chris, arrived here alone, then found an unconscious stranger on the beach and took him home to keep?"

"Sort of." Olivia wrinkled her nose. "It wasn't

quite like that."

"Well, what was it like? It sounds like that to me." Jess was becoming agitated. "Liv, you've done some daft things in your time, but this takes the biscuit. He could be anyone. You don't know him from Adam."

"I *am* Adam."

"Yes, I realised the irony as soon as I'd said it." Jess frowned at him. "But you could be anyone. How does she know you're not a criminal?"

"Hence the jokes about serial killers." Adam grinned at her. "Honestly, I'm quite safe. You can Google me, if you like."

Jess looked at him in surprise. "Why? Are you famous or something?"

"No, but remember I said I worked for Munro Solutions? Well my name is Adam Munro. My father owns the company and I'm the managing director of the UK side of the business."

Jess's mouth dropped open. "Good god. But what were you doing on the beach unconscious?"

"I slipped on a rock."

"Well, that's not really what I meant, but never mind." She regarded them seriously. "So this is all pretend, then? All for show?"

"Yes." Olivia nodded.

"Are you sure?"

"What d'you mean?"

"Well, no one could see you kissing just now. It looked to me that you were doing that for pleasure."

"We were practising." Adam smiled angelically at her, his arm sliding around Olivia's waist and pulling her close. "We want to make it believable that we're really going out."

"Well, you certainly have everyone fooled." Jess shook her head. "My problem was I didn't believe you were Chris. So you were practising last night in bed too, were you? I assume you shared a bed?"

"Well…" Olivia shuffled her feet in the sand. "There wasn't any choice, really. We didn't have sex, though, whatever Sarah says."

"And the night before, I slept downstairs on the sofa." Adam added for clarification.

"Oh, god, you stayed the night before? Liv you let a complete stranger stay in a remote cottage with you on your own? Are you mad?"

"It's okay. She wedged a chair under the bedroom door handle so I couldn't get in to murder her." Adam's eyes were glinting. "We did the same thing this morning to keep Sarah out."

"Please don't tell the others, Jess." Olivia was pressed up against Adam, her arm around his waist. "It's only for a couple of days."

"So what happened to the real Chris?"

"I caught him making out with some woman at a party." Olivia shrugged. "He was a loser anyway. I was only bringing him to prove I had a boyfriend. You all think I'm such a loser with men."

"Stop saying that." Adam tightened his arm around her. "They don't think that. Sarah was just being idiotic."

"Anyway, I'm pretty sure they don't think that now." Jess raised an eyebrow. "I reckon Sarah would run off with Adam, given half the chance."

"But this isn't real." Olivia looked away. "It's just pretend."

"Hmmm." Jess pulled her coat more tightly around

her. "If you say so. Listen, I'm going back to the house, getting really cold now. Sorry to have made you tell me. I won't tell the others." She started up the beach, then turned back to them. "What are you going to do when Christmas is over?"

"What d'you mean?" Olivia frowned.

"Well, if this isn't real, how are you going to explain breaking up with 'Chris'?"

"Don't worry about that." Adam smiled. "It won't be a problem."

Jess waved a hand and picked her way back towards the road, the wind blowing her hair in front of her face.

"What does that mean?" Olivia looked up at Adam.

"Never mind that now. Come here. We still have a kiss to practise." He pulled her closer and wrapped his arms tightly around her. "Maybe, finally, we can do this without interruption."

"Maybe," Olivia murmured, her lips close to his. "That would be nice."

When they finally pulled apart, Olivia's head was swimming with desire, her whole body tingling from his touch. Adam smiled down at her.

"Well, that was worth waiting for. We shall have to practise the neck rubbing later."

"That would be lovely." Olivia let go of him and turned away. "But no one's going to see that. How will that help the pretence?"

Adam came up behind her and put his hands on her shoulders. "It probably won't, but I think we should do it anyway." He turned her round to face him. "I'm getting cold. Shall we go back now?"

"Okay." Olivia nodded, her body still tingling from

his touch and her mind turning somersaults over some of the things he'd been saying.

"By the way, how long have you got the cottage for?" Adam took hold of her hand as they started back up the beach.

"Well, I can have it until the thirtieth, but the others all have to leave the day after tomorrow. I shall probably go then too. Not much point staying here on my own."

"Why don't we both stay for a few more days?"

"What, you and me? Together? Just us?"

"God, this is like the trip to Costa!" Adam chuckled. "Yes, you and me, together, on our own. Now you know I'm not going to murder you."

"Why?"

"Well, I thought it might be nice." Adam shrugged. "But if you don't agree…"

"Of course it would be nice." Olivia let the words out without thinking. "It would be lovely. But we will have stopped pretending then. The others will have gone."

Adam's face was inscrutable as he looked at her. "They will, but what d'you say? It might be fun."

"I suppose it might." Olivia's head was spinning as she tried to work out what he meant. He was suggesting they stay together in the cottage after the others had gone. Did that mean he wanted to spend time with her? Not just pretending to be Chris? Did that mean he actually liked her? She sneaked a glance up at him. He was watching her closely, his hand gripping hers tightly. "Okay, then. It could be fun. But shouldn't you get back to your girlfriend?"

"That's over. I told you that."

"But you haven't told *her* yet."

"I'm sure she's guessed, but you're right." He sighed. "I do have to deal with it. But it can wait another couple of days. I really don't want to think about that now." He looked down at her again. "I'm enjoying being here with you. Let's make that last as long as we can."

Olivia smiled back at him. "Okay. I'm enjoying it too. Especially the practising. But once the others have gone, we'll have no need to practise."

"I'm sure we can find an excuse."

They had reached the garden gate, and Adam held it open for Olivia to go through. She marvelled again at his impeccable manners. He was so different from the boys she usually dated. Although of course she wasn't really dating him. She glanced up at him. Or was she? She was beginning to lose track of reality.

"D'you think the others will have woken up?"

"I hope not." Adam grimaced. "It would be particularly nice if Sarah was asleep."

"What would you like to do now?" Olivia pushed open the back door.

"Something we really can't do in front of the others."

She turned round to look at him, but his face had an innocent expression on it, and he raised his eyebrows at her. Giving him a suspicious look, she kicked off her boots and went through into the kitchen. Jess was making tea, and Sarah was perched on the work surface watching her.

"There you are. You've been ages. Jess has been back for hours." She looked at them with narrowed eyes. "You didn't have sex on the beach, did you?"

"What's wrong with you, Sarah?" Olivia went over to the sink and washed her hands. "You're obsessed with sex. And no, of course we didn't. It's freezing out there."

"Well, it might have been a good way to keep warm." Adam had come up behind her and put his hands on her shoulders. "Maybe we should try that next time."

"D'you want tea, you two?" Jess was getting the mugs out.

"Please, I need something to warm up with." Olivia dried her hands and shivered. "I actually think it's getting colder. D'you think it might snow?"

"Not a chance." Adam shook his head. "Sorry. Wrong weather conditions completely. Much more likely to rain."

"Is there anything you don't know?" Sarah was watching Adam, her eyes hungrily devouring his body. "You're really clever. However did Liv catch *you*?"

Adam turned to face her, slipping his arm around Olivia at the same time. "That sounds a bit rude," he said mildly. "Are you suggesting I'm too good for your friend?"

"No. No, of course not." Sarah's face flushed and she looked down. "Just that you're so much better than her usual boyfriends. Sorry, didn't mean to sound rotten."

"Good, because Olivia deserves the best, and if anything, I'm not good enough for her." He turned to Jess. "Let me help you carry the teas in."

Jess handed him a tray with the mugs on and smiled her thanks. "That's great. I'll bring the cake. Sarah, you can take the plates and knives."

"Have we got proper Christmas cake?" Olivia felt her spirits lift. "I forgot about cake."

"We have proper Christmas cake *and* a chocolate log." Jess grinned as she produced the latter out of a large tin. "Both courtesy of my mum."

"Your mum makes the best cakes." Olivia licked her lips in anticipation. "I'm hungry again after that walk, too."

"I hope you know what you're doing." Jess looked at Olivia seriously as she picked up the Christmas cake. "I don't want you to get hurt."

"I'm fine." Olivia picked up the other plate and turned away. "Nothing to worry about."

"I'm not sure about that."

"What d'you mean?"

"I'm not stupid, Livvy." Jess put the cake down again, leaned back against the worktop, and folded her arms. "I can see the way you look at Adam. You really like him."

"No. It's just pretence." Olivia felt her face begin to flame, and looked away.

"And," Jess went on, "I can see the way he looks at you."

Olivia turned back to her. "What d'you mean?"

"He likes you too. What are you going to do about it? If this is all just for show, what's going to happen after Christmas?" Jess looked worried. "Does he have a girlfriend somewhere else? That's what I mean. Are you going to get hurt?"

Olivia put the plate down and sighed. "He did have a girlfriend, but she's the reason he ended up on the beach. He caught her in bed with his best friend."

"Oh." Jess pursed her lips. "Okay, but is it possible

he'll forgive her?"

"No. He says not. He told me she'd done something similar before and this was the last straw. He almost seemed relieved."

"Hmmm." Jess sounded unconvinced. "Well, just you make sure he's properly finished with her before you get in too deep."

"There's nothing to get in too deep with." Olivia shrugged. "We're only pretending to have a relationship."

"You and I both know that's absolute rubbish." Jess picked up the cake again. "Just be careful." She walked ahead of Olivia into the living room and placed the cake on the coffee table.

Following in her wake, Olivia found her eyes straying to Adam, who was tending to the fire. As she watched, he straightened up and caught her eye, his face breaking into a smile. She smiled back, placed the chocolate log on the table, and walked over to join him.

"Are you okay?" He put his arm around her shoulders and pulled her close. "Was Jess warning you off me?"

"Sort of." She grinned. "Well, not really. She just doesn't seem to believe we're pretending."

"Okay." He tightened his arm around her. "I think it's time we put some of that practise to good use." He guided her over to the sofa and pulled her down next to him, immediately putting his arms around her and gently kissing her on the lips.

"Again?" Sarah rolled her eyes and prodded Olivia in the ribs. "Put him down and have some cake. Plenty of time for that tonight."

Adam let her go, and Olivia snuggled up close to

him, her head on his shoulder. "We're only kissing, Sarah. You should try it sometime. With Jon," she added quickly, seeing Sarah's face.

Jess handed her a plate with a slice of Christmas cake on, and as she took a bite she felt Adam start to run his thumb across the back of her neck again. In an instant her whole body was tingling, and she could feel her heart begin to beat faster. She glanced over her shoulder at him and shook her head, but he smiled innocently at her and kept rubbing.

"Is the cake okay, Livvy?" Jess was watching her with concern. "You look like you're going to be sick."

"No, no, I'm fine," Olivia managed as her nerve endings began to explode. "The cake's lovely."

"We should watch a film," Tom suggested, stuffing some chocolate log into his mouth.

"You know what film I haven't seen for years?" Adam looked reflective, his thumb still moving up and down her neck. "*When Harry Met Sally*. I used to love that film."

Olivia put her plate down on the table with a crash and leapt to her feet, muttering, "Sorry, feel sick." She took the stairs two at a time, fully aware of the four pairs of eyes watching her in surprise. She ran into the bathroom and slammed the door shut behind her, leaning against it with her eyes closed.

God, that had been close! One more rub and she would have come. In front of all her friends, who had no idea what was going on. How embarrassing that would have been. And then Adam's comment about *When Harry Met Sally*. She was seriously going to have to kill him later.

She sat down on the edge of the bath and took a

few deep breaths. What on earth was it he was doing to her anyway? She had never experienced anything like that before. In the privacy of her bedroom it would have been delightful, but in a room full of people eating cake, it was definitely not the thing to be doing.

"You all right?" Adam's amused voice sounded outside the door.

"What do you think?"

"Let me in. I want to apologise."

She got to her feet and unlocked the door, pulling it open and scowling at him. "Don't ever do that again in public."

He closed the door behind him and grinned down at her. "I'm sorry. I couldn't resist. I honestly didn't expect you to sit there for so long. I thought you'd probably move long before it got that 'enjoyable.' "

"Oh, so it's my fault for letting you do it, is it?"

"Well, it is, in a way," Adam pointed out reasonably. "I would have stopped if you'd moved, but you just stayed there and let me do it."

"Hmmmm." Olivia narrowed her eyes at him. "I suppose so. It was so nice, though, I guess I just sort of forgot where we were."

"Hard to do when there were four other people sitting around eating cake."

"I know, I know." She looked up at him. "Right, no more in public. Keep that one for the bedroom, okay?"

"Okay."

"Because I think we may need to practise it a bit more."

"Definitely." Adam regarded her solemnly.

"Now I'm going back downstairs again. Is it safe for me to sit next to you, or should I keep well away?"

"You can sit next to me. I promise to behave."

"You may kiss me."

"Okay. I probably will. If only to annoy Sarah."

"But nothing else."

"I promise."

Olivia opened the door and headed back downstairs, bracing herself for some awkward questions.

"Are you okay, Liv?" Sarah was watching her curiously.

"Fine, thanks. Sorry about that. Think I ate my cake too quickly. Really thought I was about to throw up." She sat back down on the sofa, and Adam joined her, slipping his arm around her shoulders. "What are we going to do now? Does anyone want to play a game again?"

"What would we all be doing for Christmas if we weren't here?" Jon raised his eyebrows. "That could be interesting."

"That's easy." Sarah yawned. "I'd be asleep on the sofa by now, and my mum and dad would be arguing about the washing up. My brother would be crying because he'd already broken most of his presents, and my gran would be snoring in the corner. This is more fun."

"Have you phoned them yet?" Jon asked.

"Yeah, called them this morning. They're fine."

"I called mine, too." Olivia giggled. "Mum was getting frazzled about the turkey, Dad was trying to keep out of her way, and Aunt Janice was pissed off and shouting her mouth off because her boyfriend didn't get out of jail in time. Pretty glad I'm here, actually."

"Have you called yours, Chris?" Jess fixed Adam with an innocent stare.

"Not yet." He shook his head. "I'll do it later."

"What will they be doing?" Sarah edged slightly closer to him, and Jon caught her arm to pull her back.

"Umm. Well, I don't really know…"

"I thought you said they were going to your uncle and aunt's for lunch, didn't you?" Olivia jumped in to help him. "The ones who live in Stratford."

"Oh, yeah. That's right. I'll call them later. I expect they'll all be asleep just now."

"It's amazing just how much of Christmas Day most people seem to miss by falling asleep after lunch. A real waste, if you ask me." Tom shook his head. "I've always thought it would be fun to go somewhere really snowy for Christmas. That would be great."

"It is." Adam nodded. "We went to Switzerland one year. It was really magical. Sleigh rides in the snow and everything."

There was a momentary silence as everyone stared at him.

"That was the year your cousin paid for the trip, wasn't it?" Olivia said quickly. "The one who had the big win on the horses?"

"Yes. That's right. My cousin. It was very generous of him."

"Wow, that sounds amazing." Sarah stared at him. "Is your cousin married?"

"Sarah!" Jess reached over and slapped Sarah's arm. "What a thing to ask with poor Jon sitting just there!"

"What? Only interested." Sarah flushed slightly and looked at Jon under her lashes. "I love you, really.

But it would be nice to have lots of money."

"Oh, he's spent it all now." Adam entered into the story. "Blew most of it on the holiday. It was years ago anyway. He doesn't usually win."

"Well, if Munro Solutions pay as well as you say"—Jess glanced over at him—"then you'll be able to take Olivia somewhere like that next year."

"Maybe I will." He tightened his arm around Olivia and smiled. "Maybe I will. Would you like that?" He looked down at her.

"It sounds wonderful."

"Jon, you should go and work for them." Sarah nodded to her boyfriend.

"Sarah, I don't work in computers. I'm a data analyst. Maybe Tom should, though."

Tom shrugged. "I've thought about it, but I don't really want to move to Bristol."

"You wouldn't necessarily have to," Adam said. "There's an office in London, too, and a lot of programming gets done there. Bristol's pretty nice, though."

"I'm not a programmer." Tom shook his head. "I'm just a systems analyst."

"Still plenty of opportunities for them." Adam shrugged. "I could put in a word for you, if you like."

"I'll think about it." Tom smiled. "Thanks, though. Much appreciated."

"This is boring." Sarah rolled her eyes. "Let's play a proper game. Truth or Dare, like Chris suggested earlier."

"Go on, then." Adam grinned at her. "You can go first. Everyone okay with that?"

"Seriously?" Olivia looked up at him. "You do

know what that is, don't you?"

"Of course I do. I suggested it before lunch. Come on, might be a laugh."

"Okay, okay." Sarah scrambled to her feet. "I'll start then…"

"I meant you can be the first victim." Adam grinned evilly. "Sit down. I've got a good question for you."

Sulkily, Sarah perched on the chair next to Jon. "Go on, then."

"Truth or dare?"

"Truth."

"Who was the last person you kissed, apart from Jon?"

"What, proper kissed, or hello kissed?"

"Proper kissed," they all chorused.

"Ummm…" Sarah chewed on her thumbnail thoughtfully. "Ummmm…well, I guess that would be Simon."

"Who's Simon, and when did you kiss him?" Adam sounded as if he was enjoying her discomfort.

"My brother Simon?" Jon was staring at her in horror.

"Maybe."

"Jesus, Sarah, really? What the hell?"

"Okay, it was meant to be a hello kiss, but we were both a bit pissed and it somehow turned into a proper kiss. Not a real snog." She turned to Jon. "And we stopped when we realised what we were doing."

"When was this?" Jon was shaking his head.

"Coupla months ago. At that Halloween party." She glanced sideways at him. "Don't be mad. We didn't mean to do it."

Jon stared at her for a moment, then burst out laughing. "I remember that party. You were well pissed, and so was Simon. I believe you, but please don't do it again. That's weird."

Olivia shook her head. "Honestly, Sarah, you're awful. Your turn to ask a question."

Sarah turned to Jon. "Okay, truth or dare?"

"Dare."

"Chicken!"

"I saw what happened to you."

"Okay, then, I dare you to…take off your trousers and dance round the room in your underwear."

Jon stood up and pulled off his trousers. "Easy. Much sooner do that than answer a stupid question." He tossed the trousers onto the chair and leapt all round the room, arriving back in front of Sarah and bowing. "That do?"

"Very good. Nice boxers, by the way."

"Thank you. Right." He pulled his trousers back on and turned to Jess. "Truth or dare?"

"Truth." Jess grinned at him nervously.

"When did you last skive off work?"

"I never have."

"What?" Sarah stared at her. "You must have done. Everyone skives sometimes."

"Honestly, I haven't."

"I think she's telling the truth." Olivia curled her feet up under her and leant against Adam. "She's very well behaved."

"Boring." Sarah lay back in her chair and closed her eyes. "Come on, I want to find out something juicy about someone."

Jess looked around the remaining people. "Okay,

then. Livvy, truth or dare?"

"Truth." Olivia took a deep breath.

"Who was the last person you had sex with?"

"Chris."

"Well, that was a stupid question." Sarah opened her eyes and frowned at Jess. "We all know that."

Jess was watching Olivia. "Just checking."

"Waste of a question," Sarah muttered, closing her eyes again.

Olivia turned to Tom. "Truth or dare?"

"Dare."

"Okay. I dare you to eat a mince pie with salt and vinegar on."

"Yuck." Jess shuddered. "Go on, Tom, let's see you do it."

Tom grinned and got to his feet. He disappeared into the kitchen, reappearing moments later with a mince pie in one hand and a pot of salt in the other. "Can't find any vinegar." He shook some salt onto the pie and prepared to take a bite.

"More than that," Olivia said sternly. "Specially if there's no vinegar."

Tom shook more salt onto the pie and put it into his mouth. He closed his eyes and chewed for a moment or two. "Okay, that was gross. Need a drink of water now." He disappeared back into the kitchen and came back with a tall glass. "I don't recommend that at all. Thanks, Liv!"

"My pleasure."

Tom looked over at Adam. "Right, your turn now. Truth or dare?"

Adam looked at him thoughtfully. "Truth. I think."

"Have you ever stolen anything?"

"Pick 'n' Mix don't count," Sarah piped up from her chair.

"Not really." Adam screwed up his face, trying to remember. "Oh, when I was six I took fifty pence out of my mum's purse to buy sweets."

"Not a hardened criminal, then?" Tom said with a grin. "Nice to see Olivia's not taking after her aunt."

"Hey, not all Aunt Janice's men are criminals," Olivia objected mildly. "Just most of them."

"I can't get over how posh Chris sounds." Sarah sat up and looked over at him. "I thought you were from Essex or something. You don't sound anything like Liv or Jess."

"We moved around a lot when I was little," Adam improvised quickly. "I was born in East London, but we lived up north for a while, and down this way too. I guess it sort of evened out my accent."

"Well, it's very sexy." Sarah stood up and stretched. "Jon, you should try and talk like that."

"Are you saying I'm not sexy?" Jon grinned at her.

"No, but there's just something about a posh accent that gets me going. Chris sounds like he went to Eton or something."

"Honestly, Sarah, you do say some silly things." Olivia stood up. "I'm getting hungry again. Shall we get some snacks out? Would someone like to put some music on? That might be nice."

Chapter 7

"Well, here we are again." Adam slid into bed beside Olivia and pulled the quilt up over his shoulder. "Are you cold?"

"Freezing."

"Come on, then, let's warm each other up."

She wriggled into the middle of the bed and smiled at him. "This is becoming a habit."

"A nice one?"

"Definitely." She paused. "I do want to ask you something, though."

"Go on, then."

"What Sarah said earlier…about you talking posh. Please tell me you didn't really go to Eton."

"Of course not." Adam grinned at her. "I wouldn't be seen dead at Eton. I went to Winchester."

"Winchester! That's almost as posh!"

"To those of us who went there, it's way posher and far superior to Eton. In fact, Eton was modelled on Winchester." He grinned again and pulled her towards him. "But does it really matter where I went to school? I left nearly ten years ago. I don't care where you went."

"I went to an enormous comprehensive in Romford. Bit different."

"So? Why does any of that matter?"

"I don't know." Olivia moved a bit closer to him.

"I guess it doesn't, really. We're just so different. Our upbringings are poles apart."

"I doubt it. I'm sure we both got into trouble for the same things. Got sent to bed too early, argued with our parents, and got grounded."

Olivia grinned. "Okay, I did all those things, but my parents are a postman and a teaching assistant, and yours own a multi-million-pound computer company."

"My dad does. Mum's part owner of a chain of hotels now." Adam smiled and wrapped his arms tightly around her. "Now, I don't know about you, but I don't want our parents in here with us. How about we forget about them, and our old schools, and get on with some practising?"

"Hmmm. Okay, then." Olivia was suddenly very aware of his breath on her face. "I suppose we could. Maybe the neck thing again, now we're not in a room full of people?"

"All in good time." Adam's lips were brushing tantalisingly against her own. "Maybe some kissing first?"

"Maybe." She felt her skin tingle as his hot breath entered her mouth. "Maybe that would be nice." She pressed her lips against his, her tongue slipping into his mouth and entwining with his. He tightened his arms around her and pressed his hard body against hers.

"This would be..." Olivia muttered, her lips still pressed against his, "even better if we were naked."

"Yes." Adam put his hand up and cupped the back of her head. "It would be." As his finger started to caress the back of her neck, Olivia's body gave an involuntary lurch, and she moaned with pleasure. Adam's other hand reached down and began to gently ease her pyjama trousers down.

Her nerves jangling and her body fizzing with desire, Olivia wriggled her legs until the pyjamas lay in a heap by the bed, then reached her hand down and urgently did the same with Adam's. As their bare legs touched, she felt as if her whole body was on fire, and she pressed even harder against him.

His fingers had worked their way further down her neck and started to rub gently but vigorously in one particular spot. Olivia gasped in shock and threw her head back, her eyes screwed tightly shut and her body quivering with ecstasy. As the full force of the orgasm took hold of her, her breath came in ragged gasps and she cried out, her fingers digging into his back and her legs wrapping tightly around his.

"Oh, god," she gasped as she finally loosed her grip on him and rolled onto her back. "Oh, god, oh, god, oh, god. That was...amazing." She lay with her eyes closed, her breathing still uneven and her heart thumping uncontrollably. "What the hell were you doing? Where did you learn that?"

Adam reached over and kissed her lightly on the lips. "Glad you liked it."

She opened her eyes and stared up at him. "I'm not sure we need to practise that again. I'm pretty sure that was perfect." She smiled. "But we could always see if it can be improved."

"Olivia..." Adam ran his fingers down her cheek. "We need to talk about something."

She looked at him, her heart leaping into her throat. "Why? What about?"

"About us. About this practising we keep doing."

She felt her heart plummet as she guessed what he

was going to say. "You think we should stop?"

"I think we should stop *practising*, yes." Adam brushed her hair back from her face and looked at her seriously. "Let's be honest here. What are we practising for?"

"To make the others think we're going out." She forced the words out through dry lips.

"Okay, Well, I'm pretty sure we achieved that aim right from the start. So…why are we still practising? Are you enjoying it?"

Olivia nodded. "Yes."

"Me too. And have you been enjoying having me as a fake boyfriend?" She nodded again. "Well, how would you feel if I was your real boyfriend?"

"What?"

"We have no need to practise in order to fool your friends. In fact, they all think we're actually having sex—helped no end by your sound effects just now, I should imagine—so the only possible reason for us to be continuing to do what we're doing is because we like it." He paused and smiled at her. "And each other. So, what d'you say?"

"What?" Olivia was staring at him.

"Good god, woman, do I have to spell it out? I'm asking you out. Olivia Marshall, will you go out with me? Will you be my girlfriend—for real?"

Unaccountably, she felt her eyes fill with tears and looked away from him. "Do you really mean that?"

"Of course. Why d'you think I suggested we stay an extra few days after the others have gone?"

"Well, I did wonder." She sniffed and wiped her hands across her eyes. "I'd love to go out with you. Of course I would. But…"

"But?"

"What about Naomi?"

Adam sighed. "Yeah. I know. I need to sort that. Technically we're still going out, and I need to deal with that little issue before we can properly be together. You're right." He stroked her hair back from her face again. "I was thinking I could leave it until after we left the cottage, but now I realise I must sort it right away."

"When? Not tomorrow."

"No. Not tomorrow. It's still Christmas. Let's get Boxing Day over, and when everyone else leaves I'll go and sort things out with Naomi and then come back and join you here again. Then we can really be together. How does that sound?"

"And you really promise it's all over with her?" Olivia found her voice was shaking.

"Yes. If I'm honest, it wasn't going to last anyway. Catching her with James was just the final straw." He gave a wry smile. "I always suspected she was only after my money. I've had that problem a few times in the past."

"How d'you know I'm not after your money?"

"Because I honestly think part of you rather wishes I didn't have it." He looked down at her and laughed. "You'd prefer I was a normal person with a normal job who went to a normal school. I was worried that was all going to put you off."

Olivia smiled. "You're sort of right. It's a bit intimidating, knowing the sort of life you lead, but I can cope. But I'm definitely not after your money." She wriggled closer to him. "So if we're actually going out, how far can this practising go?"

"Not all the way yet." He looked at her seriously.

"I would like to wait until Naomi is completely out of my life before we actually have sex. Do you understand that?"

"Yes. I guess I do. How would you like to go and see her now, then?"

Adam laughed out loud. "Cheeky woman! Have patience. There are plenty of other things we can do, as you well know. The day after tomorrow, I'll be all yours."

"So are we going to tell the others, then? That you're not Chris? That's going to be weird."

"I've actually been having rather fun with that. How about we don't tell them tomorrow but leave it until everyone is leaving? We can have some fun tomorrow making up stories about Chris and his family." He sighed. "I can also imagine how even more annoying Sarah will get once she finds out who I am. She already makes it obvious she fancies me, and she'll definitely be one to have her head turned by the thought of money."

"Yeah, she will." Olivia grinned. "Okay, then, you're still Chris tomorrow, and we'll tell them all on Sunday." She wound her arms around his body. "I can't believe this is real. Why on earth would you want to go out with me? You could have anyone."

"Because you're perfect. You're beautiful, you're funny, you're brave, you're all the things I admire in people. And you're incredibly sexy, and I think we should now indulge in a bit more kissing before we go to sleep. What do you say?"

"Sounds perfect."

Chapter 8

Boxing Day

"At least no one's come banging on the door this morning." Adam rolled over and yawned. "Sarah must want a lie-in."

"Maybe we should go and wake her?" Olivia grinned over at him, marvelling again that this beautiful man would want to go out with her.

"Nah, let's enjoy the peace. What are the plans for today anyway?"

"No idea. No plans, really. Just chill and eat, I guess. There's still masses of food."

"Since I'm still pretending to be Chris today, how about telling me a bit more about him so I can make some stuff up?"

"What sort of stuff?" She peered at him suspiciously.

"Oh, I dunno, just things he may have done, places he's been. Since it doesn't really matter if we get found out now, I thought we could have some fun with it."

"Okay." Olivia chuckled. "Well, he left school after his GCSEs and went to work in a supermarket, stacking shelves."

"Seriously?"

"I told you he was an underachiever. He got bored with that and somehow ended up in some office doing the data processing thing. I never did really know what it was."

"Okay. And he has one brother? What does he do?"

"Nothing. He's on the dole. Lies on the sofa all day watching TV. His mum runs around after him, apparently. I haven't actually met any of them, so you can make stuff up if you like."

Adam rolled onto his side and propped his head up on his hand. "You're very beautiful."

Olivia glanced at him. "I'm not. I'm very ordinary. You're just being nice."

"You're going to have to learn to accept compliments if you're going out with me." He rolled over and swung his legs out of bed. "You'll be getting a lot of them. Come on, let's go and get today over with. See if you can think of any more silly games we can play."

Olivia watched him as he grabbed his towel and headed for the bathroom. She was still finding it hard to believe that he really wanted to go out with her. For real. Not just pretending to be her boyfriend but actually being a couple. She wriggled further down in the bed and stared up at the ceiling. He was so different from any of her previous boyfriends, in a very good way. And he thought she was beautiful. No one had ever said that to her before. She still wasn't sure she believed him, but it had been nice to hear.

Throwing back the quilt, she clambered out of bed and shivered. The upstairs really hadn't warmed up at all, despite the woodburner being kept alight. She picked up a jumper and pulled it over her head while she waited for the bathroom to become free, then rifled through her clothes, trying to decide what to wear.

By the time Adam returned, she had plumped for jeans and a bright blue stripy jumper.

"Not dressing up today, then?" He dumped his towel on the floor and started to peel off his pyjamas.

"No, one day was enough for that." Olivia smiled. "Need to be able to slob a bit today."

Adam fished in his carrier bags and pulled out a new pair of faded jeans, a black T-shirt, and the check shirt he had worn on Christmas Eve. "Will these do, then?"

"Perfect. Very sexy." Olivia blew him a kiss and escaped out of the room to the bathroom.

****

By the time they had all assembled downstairs, it was nearly midday, and Sarah made straight for the fridge.

"Time for wine." She peered in and frowned. "There doesn't seem to be much left."

"Well, if there isn't, it's your fault." Olivia peered around her. "We brought masses. Look, there's still that bottle of Prosecco I brought, and two more bottles of ordinary wine. What's your problem?"

"Liv, there are six of us. That won't go far."

"I have more in my room." Jess had joined them. "Livvy warned me you might drink it all. Personally, I'd like a coffee now. Anyone else?"

"Please, that would be lovely." Olivia watched as Jess retrieved the mugs from the dishwasher. "What does anyone fancy doing today, then?"

"Eating and drinking."

"Yeah, we know what you want, Sarah. Jess?"

"Play some more games, maybe? Watch a film?"

"We could play Never Have I Ever." Adam strolled into the kitchen and leaned against the worktop.

"You seem determined to embarrass us." Jess glanced over her shoulder. "But that can be fun. I'm game."

"Shall we play for money rather than drinking?" Sarah had poured herself a glass of wine. "Since Chris seems to have so much, maybe we can win it off him."

"Just pennies, then." Olivia rolled her eyes. "Chris may have money, but I don't!"

"Well, you say that." Adam grinned. "I have no cash at all. Just credit cards."

"We'll play for peanuts or something." Jess handed Olivia and Adam their mugs of coffee and picked up two more. "Come on, then, let's have a go. I'd certainly like to learn more about Chris."

Olivia glanced at her and was rewarded with an innocent look. She really hoped Adam would be careful what he said.

"Here you go, boys." Jess handed coffees to Jon and Tom. "We've decided we're going to play Never Have I Ever. You up for it?"

"Cool." Tom took the mug and gave Jess a kiss on the cheek. "Might be fun. What are we playing with?"

"Chocolates!" Olivia picked up the large box of Quality Street that Jess and Tom had brought and held it out. "Everyone take about ten chocolates, and we'll start from there." She sat down on the sofa and curled her legs up under her.

Adam had gone over to tend to the fire, and she was hoping he'd come and sit by her when he was done. While she was watching him, Sarah plonked herself down next to her.

"Think we'll keep the love birds apart this morning," she said with a grin. "We all know what a good time you had in bed last night, so you can have a bit of time apart today. Chris, you can sit over there."

Olivia felt her face begin to flame and looked away in embarrassment. She'd really have to make sure they didn't do that again tonight. Save it for when they were alone. She glanced over to the fire and caught Adam's eye. He smiled at her and winked, making her stomach do a little flip. She smiled back, suddenly feeling like a teenager again.

"Okay, are we ready? Chris, have you finished with the fire?" Jess was in organisational mood and placed her pile of sweets on the coffee table in front of her.

"Yep, I'm ready." Adam sat down opposite Olivia and took his handful of chocolates. "Who's going to start?"

"It was your idea, so you go first." Jess nodded to him.

"Okay, then. Never have I ever...been to Southend."

"Seriously?" Jess leaned forward and put one of her sweets in the middle. "Everyone's been to Southend."

"Actually, Jon and I haven't either." Sarah shook her head. "But I'm surprised Chris hasn't, since he's from Essex."

"It's more London, actually, and we never really went to the seaside when I was a kid. I knew Olivia had been there, so I was pretty sure of one chocolate."

Olivia added her chocolate to the pile, as did Tom, and Adam scooped them up. "Who's next? Are we going clockwise?"

"Yes, me next." Jess thought for a moment. "Never have I ever…been to the Ritz."

Adam tossed a chocolate over to her with a grin. "That's cheating."

"No, it's not. You knew Liv had been to Southend. Anyone else?" She glanced around. "Okay, Tom, you next."

"Never have I ever eaten squid."

"Yuck." Sarah wrinkled her nose. "I should think not. It looks ghastly."

Adam tossed him a chocolate. "I'm going to be out first at this rate."

"I've had squid." Olivia placed her chocolate on the table. "I won't do it again, but I have tried it."

"Jon next."

Jon closed his eyes. "Ummm…okay…never have I ever been in a helicopter."

"Well, that's not going to get you many sweets!" Sarah looked at him in surprise. "You should pick something one of us may have done."

Adam threw him a chocolate and shrugged.

"You *are* going to lose this." Jess grinned at him. "Is there anything you haven't done?"

"A few things, but I doubt they'll come up today." He raised his eyebrows at her.

"When did you go in a helicopter, then, Chris?" Tom was looking at him with interest.

"At a fair, when I was twelve," Adam lied smoothly. "Just a five-minute ride."

"My turn, my turn." Sarah looked round at them all. "Let's see…never have I ever had sex on a boat."

"Dear god." Adam tossed her a chocolate and sat

back in his chair. "Please tell me I'm not the only one who's done that?"

"No, not this time." Jess threw a sweet to Sarah and glanced at Tom. "Go on, you too."

Tom grinned and handed over his chocolate. "That was fun. We must do it again."

Olivia glanced over at Adam and raised her eyebrows. "So who was that with, then, Chris?" she asked innocently.

"Just a previous girlfriend. I'm sure we can do it sometime too. If you want to."

"Come on, Liv, it's your go." Sarah nudged her. "Stop getting jealous. You can hardly expect to be his first girlfriend."

Olivia sighed. "Okay, then. Never have I ever been up the Eiffel Tower."

Adam sighed again and threw her a chocolate. "I shall be out before the next round at this rate."

Olivia grinned. "I'm sure you can think of something we've all done, for next go." She picked up the chocolates from Jess, Tom, and Sarah and added them to her pile. "That was a good one. It's your go again, Chris."

Adam frowned. "Okay, maybe this will catch some of you. Never have I ever had a student loan."

"Okay, you got us all with that one!" Olivia chuckled and handed over her chocolate. "That's pretty much won back what you lost so far."

"How did you avoid a student loan?" Sarah threw the chocolate so it landed on his crotch.

"Chris left school after GCSEs," Olivia said quickly so as to avoid Adam making up an even more bizarre story. "He didn't go to Uni."

"And now you're richer than any of us." Sarah shook her head. "I told my mother I didn't need to stay on at school."

"That depends what you want to do, of course." Tom looked at Adam quizzically. "Intrigued as to how you got to be a programmer without a degree. I thought that was essential."

"Oh, I did a few courses while I was working." Adam waved a hand in the air. "Had a few contacts."

"Okay, who's next?" Olivia attempted to steer the conversation away from Adam. "Come on, Jess, it's you now."

Jess narrowed her eyes. "Right. Never have I ever pretended to be someone else."

Olivia caught her breath and stared at her in shock. Why would Jess be trying to catch Adam out? She would need to have words with her afterwards.

"That's a silly one," Sarah objected. "You won't get much from that."

"I have," Adam leant forward and handed her a chocolate. "I once pretended I was from America to impress a girl, and talked with an accent all evening."

"When was that?" Sarah laughed.

"When I was about sixteen. It didn't work. She still didn't like me."

"I pretended to be my brother to get into a film when I was younger." Jon grinned. "I used his ID."

"Oh, actually, me too." Olivia laughed. "I forgot that. I used Claire's ID to get into a club."

"There, see? I did okay with that one." Jess gathered up her winnings with a smirk. "You never know what people might have done."

Tom glanced round at them. "Here's a good one.

135

Never have I ever eaten custard."

Five chocolates appeared on the table in front of him.

"Why?" Sarah stared at him.

"I don't like it."

"Well, how do you know that if you've never had it?"

"I hate the smell so much I wouldn't even try it." He picked up the chocolates. "It comes in very handy for times like this."

"Well, I can't contend with that." Jon shook his head. "But how about this. Never have I ever eaten caviar."

Olivia tossed him a chocolate. "Had some at a wedding once. It's quite nice."

Adam put his chocolate on the table. "Me too."

"And me." Jess added hers. "I wasn't keen on it, though."

"Well, I haven't." Sarah screwed up her nose. "It's fish eggs. You do know that, don't you? That's too weird. Right, my go. Never have I ever..." She grinned evilly. "Never have I ever fallen off a rock and banged my head."

"Okay." Adam held his hands up. "You're all out to get me, I realise that. Here you go." He threw a chocolate to Sarah. "No one else would obviously be as stupid as me."

"Sarah, that was mean." Olivia frowned at her. "You knew it would only be Chris."

"Actually, it's not just him." Tom looked a bit sheepish. "I did that when I was ten." He tossed a chocolate onto the table. "Bloody hurt, too."

"Thanks, Tom." Adam grinned at him. "I don't feel

quite so idiotic now. Although you were only ten and I'm twenty-seven."

"Twenty-seven?" Jess looked at him innocently. "I thought Livvy said you were twenty-eight."

"I'm nearly twenty-eight." He smiled at her.

"Really, Jess? Does it matter?" Olivia was feeling stressed. "It's my turn now. Never have I ever been to Italy." Five chocolates appeared on the table in front of her, and she smiled. "Thought that would be a winner."

"Would you like to go?" Adam was watching her.

"I'd love to. Just never got round to it. I'd particularly love to go to Venice."

"I'll take you for your birthday."

"What?"

"I'll take you to Venice for your birthday. It'll be fun."

Olivia stared at him. It was going to be interesting going out with Adam. She would never know what was coming next. "Okay. I'll keep you to that."

"That's two rounds we've played now." Sarah stretched. "I'm getting bored. Can we get some food?"

"Yeah, let's." Jess got to her feet. "Let's see what we have left." She headed for the kitchen, followed by Sarah, Jon, and Tom.

Olivia looked over at Adam. "Venice?"

"Why not?" He shrugged. "You'd like to go, and I'd like to take you." He got up and moved over to sit on the sofa next to her. "We can do things like that, you know. We *are* going out."

"Yeah. Jess is really trying to catch you out. D'you think we should tell her the truth?"

"If you like. Maybe she'd let up on me then."

Olivia leant her head on his shoulder. "By the way,

a helicopter? I'm sure it wasn't true what you said, so when did you go in a helicopter?"

Adam looked a bit sheepish. "This is going to sound really grand, so you probably won't like it."

"Try me. I'm beginning to realise I should expect anything from you."

"Well, you know I told you I live about twenty miles from here…" She nodded. "And, as you may have noticed, that's quite a long way from Bristol. About an hour and a half by car, which is okay most of the time, especially when I stay there during the week." He paused. "But sometimes I'm needed in a hurry at work, and they send the helicopter for me."

"Oh, dear god." Olivia closed her eyes. "This really is going to take some getting used to. Does that happen often?"

"Not really, but it has happened a few times."

She peeped up at him. "Can I have a ride in it?"

"Of course you can." He put his arm around her and pulled her closer. "And we can have sex on my boat."

"*Your* boat? Oh, god, you have a boat, as well?"

"Yeah. It's moored down at Plymouth."

"And who was it you've already had sex with on it?"

"Do you really need to know that?" He looked down at her. "You'll just get cross."

"No, I won't." She shook her head. "I'm not stupid. We only started going out last night. Who was it?"

"Naomi." He made a face. "And a few others."

"A few others? How many others?"

"Look, I've had the boat since I was twenty-one. It was a pretty good place to take girls if I was trying to impress them." He gave a wry grin. "Unfortunately, most of them were more impressed with the boat than with me."

Olivia giggled. "Serves you right. Okay, I suppose I can understand that. How long have you been with Naomi?"

"Two years, off and on."

Olivia was silent, desperately trying not to imagine him having sex with the faceless girls he was trying to impress. Although why he needed to work at that she couldn't imagine. In her eyes, he was perfect and certainly didn't need a boat or a helicopter to get her attention.

"Olivia? Are you mad at me?"

"Of course not. Just trying not to think about you having sex with other people when we haven't even done it yet."

"About that." Adam smiled at her. "I think maybe we'd better lay off the neck thing until we're alone. Based on what Sarah said."

"Definitely." Olivia felt herself blushing. "I hadn't realised I was so noisy. I'm sorry."

"Don't be silly. I think it's lovely, but probably better when we're alone. Now come on, let's go and help with the food, or Sarah will think we're at it again."

"Can't wait to see her face tomorrow when we tell her who you really are." Olivia chuckled as she got to her feet. "That's going to be fun. One other thing, though. About the student loan thingy. I realise you wouldn't have needed a loan with your dad being so rich, but you did go to Uni, didn't you?" She rolled her eyes. "Oh, god, you're going to say you went to Oxford or Cambridge, aren't you?"

Adam laughed. "I may be rich, but you also need to be really clever to go there. I went to St Andrew's."

"Huh. Next poshest, I guess. Prince William went there."

"Yeah, but not at the same time. Now stop worrying about stupid things, and let's go and help the others."

****

"What's everyone doing for New Year's?" Sarah popped an olive into her mouth. "Jon and I are going to a party at his brother's house."

"Not sure we are any more." Jon grinned at her. "Not after your revelation about Halloween."

"Oh, you know that was a mistake." Sarah rolled her eyes. "I won't kiss him again. It wasn't very nice anyway."

"We're going to a party at the pub down the road from my Mum's." Jess poured a glass of wine. "It may be lame, but it's worth a try."

"I'm not going out." Olivia shrugged. "It's all so boring. I'm going over to Mum and Dad's for the night."

"No, you're not." Adam slipped his arm round her shoulders. "I'm taking you to a party at the Ritz."

"What is it with you and the Ritz?" Sarah stared at him. "That sounds very posh."

"Yeah, it is pretty smart. You'll need an evening dress," he advised Olivia.

"Will you be wearing a tux?" Olivia looked up at him with a smile.

"I will."

"Sounds lovely." She laid her head on his shoulder.

"I shall need a new dress, though."

"How come you're going to something that posh?" Jon looked over at them with interest.

"Oh, it's a work do." Adam shrugged dismissively. "They're a pretty good company to work for."

Olivia smothered a smile and snuggled closer to him. "Well, I can't wait," she said, glancing over at Jess, who was watching them closely.

"Well, you two win the prize for the best New Year plans." Sarah looked a little sulky. "P'raps you can get us invites next year, Chris."

"They may not be together next year." Jess's voice had a slight edge to it.

"Oh, we will." Adam bent down and kissed Olivia on the lips. "We will."

Chapter 9

Sunday 27ᵗʰ December

"Livvy, Livvy? Are you awake?" Jess's voice had a hint of urgency in it, and Olivia pulled open the bedroom door in surprise.

"Of course. We were just coming down. What on earth's the matter?"

"There's some girl here. She wants to see Adam."

"What?" Olivia felt her heart turn over. "What girl? What did she say?"

"She just asked to see him." Jess peered round Olivia. "Adam, can you come and talk to her?"

"Long blonde hair and a fake tan?" Adam sighed and finished buttoning his shirt.

"Yeah. Bit of an attitude, too." Jess nodded. "She was a bit rude."

"Naomi."

"How does she know you're here?" Olivia found her voice was shaking. "Adam, how could she have found you? What will you say to her?"

"What I told you I'd say to her." He moved across the room and put his hands on her shoulders. "Stop worrying. It's over between us. This actually makes things easier. I won't have to go and see her now, and we can stay here together."

"What?" Jess was looking from one to the other of

them. "Are you two…?"

"Yes. We're actually going out for real. We were going to tell you all today, before you left, and then we're going to stay on for a few days."

"Well, I thought you should be." Jess grinned. "But you'd better go and sort that girl out first."

Adam gave Olivia a quick kiss on the lips, then left the room and headed down the stairs. Olivia and Jess followed him, and Olivia saw the girl standing in the middle of the living room. She was tall, with very long straight blonde hair, and as Adam had said, a very fake tan. She was wearing skinny jeans and a long jumper, teamed with rather inappropriate high heels.

"Adam, darling. I'm so sorry." She stepped forward as he reached the bottom of the stairs and held out her arms. "Please forgive me."

"No, Naomi. Not this time." Adam stayed where he was and stared at her. "It's over. You know that. I don't trust you, and to be honest, when I think about it, I don't love you either. This has been coming for a while. I was going to come and see you later today. I'd like you to move out of the house as soon as possible." He paused. "How did you find me?"

"I tracked your phone. It wasn't difficult." She took a step closer to him. "Please, Adam, you know you don't mean that. We can work this out. It was all a mistake with James. It wasn't what you thought."

"Really?" His tone was derisive. "You were lying naked in bed with my best friend lying naked beside you. What was going on, then? A chat about the weather? Do you honestly think I was born yesterday? Now go, now, and get out of my house as fast as you can. I'll be back in a couple of days, and I expect you and all your stuff gone by then." He turned away.

"But…but you can't do that." Naomi's face blanched and a look of panic crossed it. "You can't throw me out. We talked about getting married. We have to get married."

"You should have thought of that before you fucked my friend." Adam's voice was harsh. "Of course we're not getting married. And for your information, we never were. That was all in your mind."

There was a slight pause; then Naomi cleared her throat. "But I'm pregnant."

"What?" Adam turned slowly back to face her, his eyes dark. "What did you say?"

"I'm pregnant. With your baby." Her face was ashen. "You have to marry me."

"You're lying." He stared at her with dislike. "You're just trying to get me to stay with you. Why should I believe you?"

"Because it's true." Her voice became more shrill. "Why would I lie about something like that? Look." She fished in her pocket. "Here's the test I did." She held out a long white plastic stick. "Now you have to believe me."

Still standing on the stairs, Olivia found she was holding her breath, and her head began to spin. She sat down abruptly, and Jess materialised beside her and took her hand.

Slowly Adam reached out and took the pregnancy test. He stared at it. "How do I know it's mine?" His voice was subdued.

"Of course it's yours. James was just a one-off. A mistake. I'm sorry."

"You slept with James while knowing you were

pregnant?"

"No. No. Of course not." Naomi tossed her hair back in annoyance. "I didn't know then. I only found out this morning."

"I'm sorry, Naomi, but I'm finding this very hard to believe." Adam ran a hand through his hair. "You must see it from my point of view. I find you having sex with my best friend and leave. Then next time I see you, you claim to be carrying my baby. Bit of a coincidence, I feel."

Naomi was staring at his forehead, revealed when he moved his hair. "What happened to your head?"

"I slipped on a rock." Adam shook his head. "But never mind that. Why should I believe you?"

"Look at the test, Adam. It's positive. What more proof do you want? I love you. I'm sorry. Please come home and we can work this out."

Adam stared at her for a moment. "Sit down and stay there." He pointed to the sofa. "I have to do something." He turned back to the stairs. "Jess, please will you stay with her, keep an eye on her? I need to talk to Olivia."

Jess nodded and moved off the stairs and into the living room.

Adam caught Olivia's hand and pulled her back upstairs with him. He went into the bedroom and closed the door behind them.

"Shit." He sat down on the end of the bed and put his head in his hands. "I never thought she'd try something like this." He looked up at Olivia. "I am so sorry. So sorry. I have to sort this out."

"Is it true?" Olivia found her voice was almost inaudible, and tears were building up behind her eyes.

145

"No. I'm sure it's not true." Adam pulled her down beside him. "I'm quite sure she's lying. But I need to be able to prove it. Get her to admit it." He looked at her sadly. "I'm going to have to go back with her until I can sort it out. Do you understand?"

"But she has a positive pregnancy test."

"Which may not even be hers, for all we know. She has some very devious friends. Or she may be pregnant and it's not mine. I will find out the truth. But Olivia…" He took her hands in his and looked her in the eyes. "I will *not* get back together with her. She can't blackmail me like this. I don't love her, and I want to be with you. If you still want me?"

"Of course I do." She nodded, a tear trickling down her cheek. "But could she be pregnant? How can you be sure?"

"I'm sure." Adam's face was hard. "We always took precautions, and to be honest, she's always said she didn't want children for years yet. She's lying, and I'll find out. But it may take a few days." He pulled her close and pressed his lips into her hair. "I'm so sorry. What will you do? Will you stay here? I don't know how long I'll be."

She shook her head. "No. I'll go home. I may go to my parents' for a few days. I'm going there for New Year anyway. I'll be okay."

"I'm taking you out at New Year. I told you that."

"Was that real? I thought you were making that up."

"No. Of course not." He pulled back and looked down at her. "When will you get it? I really like you. I really want to take you on dates you'll like, and that can start with New Year's Eve."

"Okay. But I will go to my parents', in case you're not finished with Naomi. In case something goes wrong."

"Nothing will go wrong."

"If she really is pregnant and it's yours, then what?"

"That won't happen. Everything will work out." He leaned forward and kissed her gently on the mouth. "Don't worry, and I'll see you in a few days, or sooner hopefully."

He stood up and gathered up his belongings into the plastic bags, then with one last look at her, he left the room, letting the door swing shut behind him.

Olivia sat silently on the bed for a moment, then let herself fall backwards and covered her face with her hands. She knew it had been too good to be true. Whatever he said, she had a very bad feeling about it, and she had a nasty suspicion that Naomi had been telling the truth.

If that was the case, she felt that Adam might see it as his duty to marry her. From what she knew of him so far, she had determined that he was an honourable person, and that was the sort of thing he would do. He wouldn't want to, and she did believe he wanted to be with her, but he might feel he had to.

She rolled onto her stomach and wiped her eyes. She needed to face the fact that it might all be over. That might be the last she saw of him. And all she could do was go home, or to her parents', and wait for him to call her.

In an instant her whole body went hot and cold with shock. They hadn't exchanged phone numbers. He had no way to contact her. She sat up abruptly and leapt off the bed. Maybe she could catch him before he left. She pulled open the bedroom door and came face to face with Jess.

"Have they gone?" She almost screamed the words.

Jess nodded. "Yeah, they just drove off."

"Shit." Olivia turned back to the bed and punched at the pillow viciously. "We forgot to exchange phone numbers. He can't contact me. Jess, what shall I do? He can't contact me and I can't contact him. Jess, help me!"

Jess closed the door and sat down on the bed, pulling Olivia down beside her. "Stop panicking. He'll find you. Naomi found him. He'll find you somehow." She put her arm around Olivia's shoulders. "And you know where he works. You can always call there."

"No, I couldn't." Olivia shook her head decisively. "He's the managing director. I can't just call him, and he said the office is closed until after New Year. Anyway, he has to sort this out first. I won't know when he's done it, and I don't want to hassle him. Jess, this is awful."

"Yes, it is rather." Jess sighed. "But he did seem pretty sure she was lying, and I must say I didn't like her much." She nudged Olivia. "And to be honest, I could see he really does like you. Try not to worry. It may take him a day or two, but I'm sure it'll work out and he'll find you." She smiled. "He works with some of the most sophisticated computer systems in the world. If they can't track someone down, I don't know what could."

Olivia looked at her sadly. "Jess, he's only known me for three days. He's been with her for two years. If

148

she really is pregnant, he's going to feel he has to do the honourable thing and marry her. I know he will." Her eyes filled with tears. "I wouldn't blame him. But I really do like him. You probably think I'm being ridiculous, but I thought he might be the one."

"And he probably still is." Jess took her by the shoulders and shook her gently. "She looked like a right scheming bitch to me. I'm sure she's making it up. Probably out to get his money."

Olivia nodded. "He said he thought she was. He says he's had a lot of problems with that."

"Well, there you go, then." Jess patted her on the back. "Cheer up and come downstairs. You're going to have to explain it all to the others, I'm afraid. They appeared just as Adam was leaving. I'll help." She stood up and pulled Olivia to her feet. "Come on, I'm sure it'll work out. Are you still staying on here after we've gone?"

"No. I told him I'd go home and probably go to my parents'. I don't know how long he needs, and I'd just fret if I was here alone."

"Good." Jess nodded as she ushered her through the door. "I was actually going to insist you didn't stay. You must come to mine tonight. No arguments."

"Okay." Olivia managed a small smile. "I guess that would be nice."

As they reached the bottom of the stairs, Olivia found three pairs of puzzled eyes fixed on her. She took a deep breath, walked over to the sofa, and curled up in the corner, waiting for someone to say something.

"Liv? What's going on?" Sarah broke the silence. "Where has Chris gone, and who was that tart?"

Despite her mood, Olivia couldn't help a small

smile curling the corners of her mouth. "Tart" seemed like a good way to describe Naomi. Yeah, she liked that. She sighed.

"Okay, here's the whole story. That wasn't Chris, that was Adam. And the tart was Adam's ex-girlfriend."

There was a stunned silence.

"What?" Sarah stared at her. "That wasn't Chris? What d'you mean?"

Olivia sighed again. "Chris and I broke up, coupla days before Christmas, and I came down here alone on the twenty-third. I went for a walk and found Adam unconscious on the beach."

"So you brought him home and kept him?" Sarah's voice was confused.

"That's what I said." Jess grinned.

"You knew?" Tom stared at Jess.

"I thought something didn't seem right. He wasn't anything like the Chris she had described to me, so I followed them to the beach on Christmas Day and made them tell me. They asked me to keep it quiet for now."

"But why did you say he was Chris?" Sarah looked even more confused.

"Actually, I didn't." Olivia shrugged. "If you remember, you assumed he was Chris and said something about thinking I'd made him up. That annoyed Adam, and without really thinking it through, he went along with it and let you think he was Chris. Once he'd done that, it would have been difficult to say he wasn't, so we went to the shops, bought him some clothes, and I told him a bit about the real Chris and a bit about me, so he'd know what he was talking about."

"So he's not really a rich computer programmer, then?" Sarah looked disappointed.

"Oh, yeah, that bit's real. That was Adam. Chris is a data entry processor, but Adam said he didn't know what that was and insisted on saying he was a computer programmer."

"So he really works for that Munro firm, then?"

"Well, what he didn't tell me when we went shopping was who he was. His name is Adam Munro, and his father owns Munro Solutions. So yes, Sarah, he is rich. Very rich."

"And you just found him on the beach? Wow. But you two were obviously doing it. That's not like you, Liv. You hardly know him."

"That was all for show. And we didn't have sex."

"Rubbish." Sarah shook her head. "No way was that just for show. You were *so* into each other. It was obvious. And I heard you have sex. We all did."

Olivia felt her face flush and looked down at her hands. "Okay, we are into each other, and on Christmas night he asked me out for real." She glanced up. "We thought we'd keep it to ourselves until this morning, and then tell you all. It was just too complicated to explain, and we didn't want to spoil Boxing Day."

"So you did have sex."

"No."

"Liv, you were screaming. You were definitely having sex."

"I had an orgasm, but we didn't have sex." Olivia forced the words out and didn't look at them. "He did this thing…"

"It's okay, Livvy, we don't need the details." Jess jumped in. "No, Sarah, we really don't."

"So why did bitch-face turn up, and why has he gone away with her?"

"He broke up with her the day I found him on the beach. He had caught her in bed with his best friend. He said it wasn't the first time she'd done something like that, and he walked out." She paused and took a deep breath. "Today she turned up and tried to apologise, but he told her it was over. Then she…" Her voice broke, and she swallowed. "She said she was pregnant and showed him a test."

"Shit, that's a bit heavy." Jon looked upset. "Was she telling the truth?"

"Adam didn't believe her, but she insisted it was true. He went with her to sort it out." Olivia felt tears threatening again and wiped her hand across her eyes. "He still reckons she's lying and says he'll find out the truth and then come back to me." Her voice broke. "But we forgot to exchange phone numbers. He won't know how to contact me."

"Yes he will," Jess cut in at once. "I told you he'll be able to find you. He knows your name, and he has the most sophisticated computer systems at his fingertips. He'll find you, Livvy, I promise."

"Maybe I should stay here in case he comes back tomorrow or something."

"You told him you were going to your parents'." Jess shook her head. "I'm not letting you stay here alone anyway. He'll find you, but it may take a day or so to sort this mess out."

Sarah was watching Olivia. "Suppose she really is pregnant. What will he do then?"

"I think he might think he has to marry her." Olivia's voice was little more than a whisper.

"That'll never happen." Sarah shook her head firmly. "Anyone could see he was mad about you, Liv.

He'll come back for you. There's no way he'll marry someone else."

"You think he likes me, then?"

"Hello! Of course he does. It was bloody obvious to all of us. You're crazy about each other. No way that was acting from either of you. And I still don't believe you didn't have sex, whatever you say. And he is *so* hot, Liv. I'm really jealous."

"I *am* here," Jon put in mildly.

"You must agree he's hot, though, Jon," Tom put in with a grin. "Even I think that."

"Hmm." Jon grunted noncommittally, and Jess looked at Tom in surprise.

"You thought so? I'm both impressed and worried," she said with a smile.

"Still not sure what to do now," Olivia commented, feeling the situation was getting away from her. "I don't even know where he lives."

"Well, even if you did, you couldn't go there while the bitch is still there. Trust him to sort it out, Liv. He'll be back." Sarah reached over and patted Olivia on the hand. "You go home, and he'll find you, just like Jess said."

"Okay, I guess you're right. It would be too depressing to stay here alone. I'll come back with you, Jess, if you really meant that?"

Jess nodded. "Of course. I have to work tomorrow, but we can have a nice evening, and you can tell me even more about him."

"I don't know all that much more about him." Olivia gave a wry grin. "He's just the stranger I kidnapped from the beach."

"The rich stranger who can give you orgasms by

some strange method."

"Stop fishing, Sarah. She's not going to tell you." Jess got to her feet. "Shall we get packed up, then? I'd like to get going in an hour or so."

Chapter 10

Olivia watched as Jess said goodbye to Tom and closed the door.

"Are you sure you didn't want to spend the evening with Tom? I don't want to be in the way."

"No, it's fine." Jess shook her head and walked into the kitchen. "We hadn't planned to spend tonight together anyway. I have to get up early for work. D'you want a glass of wine?"

"Please. That would be nice." Olivia followed her into the kitchen. Jess's flat was small but very well equipped, and Olivia always felt relaxed there. She leant against the worktop and watched as Jess poured two large glasses of white wine and rummaged in a cupboard for some snacks. "This is nice. Hadn't realised how much I didn't want to be alone tonight."

"Well, that's what I thought." Jess smiled over her shoulder at her. "If you'd geared yourself up to spending a couple of days alone with Adam, then it would feel weird." She handed a glass to Olivia, and they took them back into the living room. "It'll all work out, you know. I could tell he really liked you. Sarah was right."

"I know." Olivia sat down and curled up into the corner of the sofa. "But suppose she was telling the truth? He can't just abandon her."

"Why the hell not?" Jess looked at her in surprise.

155

"He caught her cheating. He doesn't owe her anything."

"He's too much of a gentleman." Olivia took a long slurp of wine. "He's got really good manners. I think he'd see it as his duty."

"Fiddlesticks." Jess took a handful of peanuts and tossed them into her mouth. "However polite he is, he's not going to marry a woman he doesn't love, and who cheated on him, just because she's pregnant."

"Being pregnant isn't a 'just,' Jess. It's a big deal."

"Stop worrying. You wait and see. By Tuesday you'll be wondering what all the fuss was about. He will have got rid of her and be hammering on your door, waiting to take you to the Ritz for tea, or whatever it was."

"Beginning to wish he really was a serial killer. Then he could get rid of her properly." Olivia popped a crisp into her mouth.

"About that." Jess looked at her. "Why the serial killer thing?"

"Well, when I found him, I had no idea who he was, and I said for all I knew he might be a serial killer." She smiled. "We have the same sense of humour, and we kind of played with that. I even asked him to start with Sarah."

Jess burst out laughing. "Nice one. God, she can be annoying, can't she?"

"Yeah." Olivia bit her lip and looked at Jess. "Did I really make a noise the other night?"

Jess grinned and nodded. "Oh, yeah. We assumed you were at it."

"Oh, god." Olivia put her head in her hands. "How embarrassing. Nearly as bad as…"

Jess looked at her curiously. "As bad as what?"

"Nothing."

"Livvy? Tell me."

Olivia took another long swig of wine. "Remember on Christmas Day when I ran upstairs and said I felt sick?" Jess nodded. "Well, Adam was...he was doing this thing. With my neck. He kinda rubbed it, and it nearly gave me an orgasm." She peeped at Jess from behind her wine glass. "That's what we were doing in bed."

"God, Livvy! So he nearly made you come in the living room in front of everyone? Why the hell did you let it go that far?"

Olivia sniffed. "That's what he said. He said I should have moved out the way."

"Well, I think you probably should." Jess giggled. "You are a twit sometimes. So you really haven't had proper sex yet, then?"

"No. He wanted to get Naomi completely out of his life first. Now I wish we'd done it, just in case he doesn't come back."

"He will come back." Jess took some more peanuts. "Just be patient."

Olivia finished her wine and placed the glass on the table. "He's so different from other people." She smiled at Jess. "He really could take me to Venice for my birthday without batting an eyelid. In fact, we'll probably go by helicopter, or on his boat."

"He has his own helicopter?" Jess stared at her in amazement.

"Well, no, it belongs to the company, but they use it to pick him up for work if he's needed in a hurry. It's so cool. He says I can have a ride in it." Her face fell, and she curled her feet even tighter underneath her.

"But that probably won't happen now. None of it will happen, and I'll never get to have sex on his boat."

"Yes, you will. Don't be so negative. If he likes you as much as it sounds, then he'll find a way to deal with the ex-girlfriend. You'll go to Venice in the summer. Wait and see."

"I hope you're right." Olivia picked up a cushion and hugged it tightly. "Is there any more wine? And can we put some music on?"

"Sure." Jess got to her feet and picked up Olivia's wine glass. "You choose the music. You know where the CDs are." She disappeared into the kitchen, and Olivia sat on the floor in front of Jess's CD collection to make her choice.

"Are you sure you don't mind what I put on?" she called as she selected a disc.

"Anything."

"Okay. I think this fits my mood." She took the disc out of the box and put it in the CD player. "Hope you don't think it's too depressing."

"Oh, god, what have you chosen?" Jess reappeared carrying the wine just as the strains of R.E.M.'s "Everybody Hurts" filled the room. She laughed. "Okay. I love that, actually, and I can see it might suit you right now. Here." She held out the wine. "D'you want a pizza or something? We could order in."

"I am a bit hungry." Olivia scrambled to her feet and took the wine. "Yeah, pizza would be nice. I'll pay. My treat for you letting me stay tonight."

"Okay." Jess shrugged. "No need, but I'm not going to turn down free food. I'll call. What d'you want on yours?"

"Anchovies and olives." Olivia curled up on the

sofa again. "And get some garlic bread, will you? Maybe we could watch a film later, too."

"Nice." Jess grinned at her. "Maybe I'll choose that. Don't want anything too depressing!"

Chapter 11

Monday 28th December

Olivia let herself into her flat and shivered. It was not nearly as well insulated as Jess's, and having not had the heating on for the best part of a week, it was like walking into a fridge. She tossed her bag onto a chair and went straight over to make a cup of coffee. That ought to warm her up. It was hardly worth putting the heating on, since she was planning to go straight over to her parents' house as soon as she had unpacked from the trip away and thrown a few things in a bag for the next few days.

She poured the boiling water into her mug and stirred in some milk. That should keep her going until she got to Romford. Her mother was bound to ply her with tea and cake, so there was no point eating now. May as well save her own food for later. She cradled the mug in her hands and perched on the edge of the sofa, her mind flitting to Adam and wondering what he was doing. Was he with Naomi? Had he managed to get her to admit she was lying? She took a long slurp of coffee. Was she lying?

She closed her eyes and thought back to their last night in bed together. He really did have the most amazing body, and the things he could do with his lips and his fingers... She shivered, as she recalled the whole neck-rubbing incident, and opened her eyes. She really mustn't think about it. If he never came back, she didn't think she could bear it. It was shocking her just how much she was missing him, after only knowing him for three days. Something had just clicked between them, and she prayed he'd be able to work things out with Naomi.

With a sigh she got up, washed her mug, left it to drain, and began to empty her bag. At the bottom she found the underwear and perfume Adam had given her for Christmas. Only three days ago, but it felt like a lifetime. She picked them up and stared at them, then carefully placed them back at the bottom of her bag. She would take them to her parents' house, just in case. Just in case what, she wasn't sure. In case he came and found her and she could wear them? Or in case he didn't come back and she could hold them? God, she was getting morbid.

In a sudden flurry of energy, she whizzed around the small flat and tossed a few clothes into her bag. No need for anything fancy. She wasn't going anywhere. She was planning on slobbing out on their sofa for a few days and being pampered by her mum. Lots of cake and tea and sympathy. Her mum was good at that. Zipping up her bag, she glanced around to make sure everything was turned off, then pulled her coat back on and left, making sure to set the burglar alarm and lock the door securely. It still astonished her how people in the country didn't feel the need to lock their doors. It was second nature to her, and she doubted she could ever get used to that.

Her car was parked just along the road, and she stowed her bag in the back and set off for Romford. It was only supposed to be about a thirty-minute drive from her home in South Woodford, but Olivia was well aware that it could take nearly twice that at certain times of the day, so she wanted to get on her way as soon as possible.

As she pulled out and joined the traffic on the A1009, she actually found herself thinking fondly of the peaceful cottage by the beach. Maybe living in the country wouldn't be that strange after all. Perhaps she should give it a try one day.

Forty minutes later, she pulled up outside the 1960s semi-detached house where she had grown up. It looked pretty much the same as it had for the last twenty-five years, and she felt a sudden sense of security that had been missing for the last twenty-four hours. She hauled her bag out of the car, locked and immobilised it, and let herself in through the back door.

"Mum? Dad? Anyone home?"

"In here, love." Her mother's voice floated through from the living room.

Olivia pushed the door open and went in. The room was lovely and warm, and her mother was curled up on the sofa reading a book and drinking tea.

"Hi, Mum. Can I stay for a few days?"

"Of course you can." Sue Marshall got to her feet and frowned. "What's wrong? Didn't Christmas go well?"

Olivia dropped her bag on the floor and burst into tears. In seconds Sue had propelled her over to the sofa and settled her in the corner, holding tightly to her hand.

"Sorry." Olivia hiccupped and buried her face in her mother's shoulder. "Sorry, just being silly."

"Nonsense." Sue stroked her hair gently. "But this isn't like you. Come on, tell Mummy all about it. It's not your break-up with Chris, is it? I didn't think that had bothered you."

"No, it's not that." Olivia sat up and wiped her hand across her eyes. "I was glad to be rid of him, actually. No. Mum, I met someone else."

"That was quick." Sue smiled at her. "Well, who is he, and why on earth are you crying? You didn't split up with him too, did you? When are we ever going to meet one of your boyfriends?"

"It's a long story." Olivia managed a smile. "You'd better make tea. And do we have cake?"

"Oh, it's like that, is it?" Sue got to her feet and hooked her long hair behind her ears. "You get comfy, and I'll get the tea and cake."

"Mum?"

Sue turned at the door. "Yes?"

"Are those my jeans?"

"Umm…well, they may be." Sue looked a little sheepish. "Well, yes, you left them here the other week, and it seemed a shame not to make use of them. They needed the exercise." With a wide grin she left the room and headed for the kitchen.

Olivia smiled to herself and curled her feet up under her. Her mother was incorrigible. Her clothes just weren't safe around her. Only last month she had had to wrestle her for the return of two of her tops. It was the curse of having a mother who still had the figure of a twenty-five-year-old. Still, at least it boded well for her when she reached her forties.

She glanced around the room. It was all so familiar: the three-piece suite they had had since she was about five, the two full-to-bursting bookcases along one wall, the French windows leading out into the tiny square garden behind the house. The only thing that was relatively new was the television. She wriggled further down among the cushions and sighed. Once she'd told her mum about Adam, it would make it all easier to deal with. Her mum always knew what to say.

"Here we go." Sue returned carrying a tray containing two steaming mugs of tea and a plate of chocolate cupcakes. "Will this do?"

"Perfect." Olivia sighed and picked up a cake. This was just what she needed. She took a sip of tea. "You really do make the best tea."

"Of course I do. Now, come on, spill. Who's this new man, and where did you find him? And more to the point, why are you sad?" Sue curled her legs up under her and got comfy.

"Well…" Olivia smiled. "Actually, I did find him. On the beach by Aunt Mary's cottage. Unconscious."

"Ooh, this is already interesting. Go on."

"I took him back to the cottage to patch him up because he wouldn't go to the hospital."

"And? What, you kept him?"

"Why do people keep saying that?" Olivia tutted with annoyance. "He stayed, but I didn't just 'keep' him. I made him stay because I didn't think he should be alone and he said he was going to a hotel."

"Didn't he have a home to go to?"

"Yes, but he wouldn't go. Long story, but he'd just found his girlfriend in bed with his best friend, so he walked out."

"Ooh, this is getting even better! Very like the book I read last week. Go on."

"Mum, honestly! This is real life. Anyway, he stayed the night with the idea that he'd leave before the others arrived in the morning."

"Hang on there." Sue held up her hand. "You were alone in the cottage? This was the first night you were there? And you let a complete stranger stay the night? Livvy, he could have been anyone, he could have been a serial…"

"Killer. Yes I know. We had this conversation. A lot." Olivia grinned. "We discussed that. That was really when we started to hit it off. We both had the same sense of humour. But anyway, yes, I let him stay, but I barricaded the bedroom door so he couldn't murder me."

"What with?"

"A chair. Look, it really doesn't matter, because he didn't murder me, and now we're going out. Or we may be."

"I feel you may be leaving some things out here. What happened when your friends arrived?"

Olivia leaned back and closed her eyes. "This is where it got a bit silly."

"Oh, like it was all totally normal up to that point?"

"Okay, even sillier. Sarah and Jon arrived really early, and Adam—that's his name—opened the door. They assumed he was Chris, so he didn't say he wasn't."

"And he did that why?" Sue had settled back and was listening avidly, sipping her tea.

"You know what Sarah can be like. Well, she announced that she'd bet Jon I'd made Chris up and that he wouldn't be there. Adam thought that was really mean, so on the spur of the moment he pretended to be

Chris."

"Ah. Nice." Sue nodded. "He sounds like a nice boy."

"He's nearly twenty-eight."

"Sweetie, I'm nearly fifty. That's a boy. Go on."

"For some reason, I decided to go along with it, so he stayed for Christmas and pretended to be Chris."

Sue narrowed her eyes. "And the sleeping arrangements?"

"Trust you to pick up on that." Olivia sighed. "Well, obviously he had to sleep in my room, but we didn't have sex." She looked away. "But we did kiss in front of the others. So it would look convincing."

"Of course." Sue nodded, and Olivia noticed her lips were twitching.

"And we practised the kissing when we were on our own. Just so we got it right."

"Naturally. As you do."

"Mum, I'm not sure you're taking this seriously."

"Well, it's not really very serious, is it? I presume the kissing went well and you ended up falling for each other? Sounds pretty fun to me."

"Well, yeah. Pretty much. We realised we really liked each other for real, and on Christmas night he asked me out."

"What about the cheating girlfriend?"

Olivia was silent for a moment. "She's the only fly in the ointment."

"He still likes her?"

"No. He hates her. He said it wasn't the first time she'd cheated and this was the final straw. He was planning to go see her yesterday and tell her to get out of his house. Then he'd come back to the cottage, and we were going to spend a few more days there alone."

"Okay. Sounds good. So what happened?"

"She turned up at the cottage, first thing yesterday morning." Olivia felt her eyes fill with tears. "He told her it was over, and she…she…"

"She what, darling?" Sue leaned forward and took her hand. "Told him she was pregnant?"

"How did you know?" Olivia stared at her in surprise.

"Standard plot in a romance novel. I expect she's lying."

"She had a test with her. It was positive."

"That doesn't mean anything. She could have got that from anyone. So where is he now? Don't tell me he thinks he has to stand by her?"

"He doesn't believe her, but he said he needed to go back with her to get her to admit she was lying. Then he said he'd come and get me."

"Well, that doesn't sound too bad." Sue smiled at her. "I'm sure she *is* lying, she would have been desperate to keep him. Desperate women try anything."

"But Mum, he doesn't know where I am. We forgot to exchange phone numbers. He may never find me."

Sue looked at her in surprise. "He knows your surname, I hope? Does he know where you live?"

"I told him I worked in a school in South Woodford and that you and Dad lived in Romford."

"He'll find you. Or maybe you could contact him? Do you know where he lives, or works?"

"Ah, yes, that's the other thing." Olivia couldn't help smiling. "I don't know where he lives, but I do know where he works. He's managing director of

Munro Solutions in Bristol. His father owns the company."

"Okay." Sue stared at her. "Well, that's nice. Better than that underachiever you were going out with last. So he's rich, then?" Olivia nodded. "So my guess is that's another reason this girl doesn't want to lose him. Trust me, darling, she's lying. I take it you don't want to contact him until you know he's sorted it?"

"I knew you'd understand. No, I think I should wait for him, but I'm really worried he won't find me."

"Of course he will. It's not that hard. Now, have another cake and tell me more about him. Is he very good-looking?"

"He's gorgeous. Dark reddish hair and piercing green eyes." Olivia took a bite of cake. "And a body to die for."

****

Olivia climbed out of the bath and reached for the big fluffy white towel hanging on the heated towel rail. That was a new addition since she had left home. She held the warm material against her face and sighed. It was nice to be home, but she was still totally consumed with worry about Adam.

Chatting to her mum had been brilliant, and she definitely felt a bit better, but until she heard from him—although how was that going to happen?—she couldn't really relax.

She towelled herself dry and pulled on her pyjama trousers and a baggy black T-shirt. No one dressed for dinner in her parents' house, and she just wanted to be comfortable. And her aunt Janice was joining them, complete with jailbird boyfriend. She couldn't help thinking that perhaps it was a good job Adam wasn't going to be there. Janice wasn't the best introduction to her family.

Hanging the towel back up to dry, she let herself out of the bathroom and ran downstairs. Her mother was stirring something in a large pan on the stove, and Janice was perched on the work surface, gesticulating wildly.

"Honestly, Sue, she was a right cow. No idea what he saw in her... Oh, hi, Liv. You okay?"

Olivia nodded to her aunt, inwardly sighing as she took in the grey tracksuit bottoms and bright pink hoodie. With her hair scraped back into a ponytail, her aunt looked like the perfect example of a chav. Yeah, she was very glad Adam wasn't meeting her today.

"Hi, Janice. Had a good Christmas?"

"No. Didn't you hear? Brian didn't get out until yesterday. Bloody typical! I never get a break." She slid down off the surface and pushed past Olivia. "Brian! Come an' say hello to Liv."

Olivia exchanged a glance with her mother, and Sue mouthed, "He'll try and kiss you. Be prepared," then went back to stirring the chilli.

Olivia shuddered and braced herself, ready for the arrival of Brian. She had met him once, before he was carted off to prison, and she hadn't been impressed. The door swung open, and she forced her lips into a welcoming smile. "Hello, Brian. Glad to see you're out."

Brian advanced towards her, arms outstretched, and attempted to plant a wet kiss on her lips. Olivia turned her head at the last minute and the kiss landed on her ear.

"Hi, Liv. Lookin' as hot as ever, then?" Brian

leered at her and ran a stubby-fingered hand over his shaved head. "Nice to see ya. You stayin' over, then?"

"Yes, just for a few days." Olivia edged backwards and took refuge behind her mother. "Probably until New Year."

"You could come out with us on New Year's, if you like." He leered at her again, appearing to speak directly to her chest. "We're going to the club. Should be a good night."

"I'm sure Olivia has plans with her friends." Sue turned off the heat under her pan. "Now go and sit down. Supper's ready. Give your dad a call, Livvy."

Olivia escaped past Brian and called up the stairs, "Dad, supper's ready." Moments later her father appeared and ran downstairs to join her. He peered into the dining room.

"Oh, god, Brian's here." He caught Olivia's hand. "If we can keep the conversation off football, he won't be able to understand us. God, what is she thinking?" He shook his head as he watched his sister-in-law wind her arms around her boyfriend's thick neck. "The man looks like a Neanderthal."

Olivia giggled. "He tried to kiss me."

"Yeah, he keeps doing that to your mum, too. She's got pretty good at avoiding him. She moved out the way yesterday and he tripped over the table and went flying." He smiled down at her. "Nice to have you home, love."

"It's nice to be home, Dad." She reached up and kissed his cheek. "You're looking nice. Have you done something to your hair?"

He put his hand up and rubbed it over his wavy brown hair. "Had a trim, nothing special."

Olivia was unconvinced but followed him into the dining room and took her seat at the table. Brian leered at her again, and she felt someone's foot press on hers. She pulled it back and wrapped her feet safely around the chair legs. God, he was disgusting. The sooner Janice dumped him the better.

"Here we go." Sue appeared and put plates of chilli and rice in front of them all. "Tuck in. There's garlic bread just coming. Paul, make sure they all have something to drink."

"I'll have a beer, mate." Brian didn't look up from shovelling chilli into his mouth. "Whatever you got."

"Yeah, me too." Janice nodded.

"I'll help you, Dad." Olivia got to her feet. "Have we got wine?"

"In the fridge. You get that for you and your Mum, and I'll get the beers."

Olivia followed him to the kitchen to fetch the drinks, passing Sue in the doorway carrying a plate of garlic bread. "He's even worse than before," Paul muttered to her as they passed. "Make her get rid of him."

Sue rolled her eyes and carried on into the dining room while Olivia and Paul sorted out the drinks.

"So what's this new young man of yours like, then?" Paul opened a can of beer and poured it into a glass.

"Not sure he's mine yet." Olivia opened a new bottle of Pinot Grigio. "But he's really nice."

"Rich too, your mother said?"

"Yeah, rich too. And pretty posh. He went to Winchester College."

"Did he, now?" Paul grinned at her. "And he wants

to go out with an Essex girl like you? Wonders will never cease."

"God, Dad, really? As if I'm not worrying about that myself. Don't you start!"

"Only joking, Livvy. You're good enough for anyone. He's a computer guy, then, is he?"

"Yeah, he was behind that new search engine—you know, Boodle Search—that came out in the summer. He's pretty clever."

"I look forward to meeting him." They carried the drinks back into the dining room and handed them out.

Brian snatched his and took a long swig. "Thank fuck. This chilli's too bloody hot for me, Sue. Don't know what you were thinking."

"Is it, Brian?" Sue took a forkful. "Strange, it's not as hot as I usually make it. Seems fine to me. Just have some bread, then."

"Don't like garlic. It gives me wind."

"That's a shame. We've got apple crumble for pudding, or does that keep you awake?"

Brian gave her a suspicious look and shovelled some more chilli into his mouth, closely followed by a long slurp of beer. His round face had gone bright red, and Janice was watching him with mild distaste.

"You look awful," she said bluntly. "I think you should go home."

"Yeah, well, this is dreadful. Sorry, Sue. Can't eat any more. Come on, then, babe, let's go." He pushed his chair back and stood up. "We can go back past the kebab place."

"No, I meant you go." Janice carried on eating. "I'm enjoying this. I'll see you tomorrow."

Brian stared at her in surprise. "What?"

"You go home. I'm staying here with my sister. I'll see you tomorrow. Maybe."

"Whadyer mean, maybe?"

"Well, I may not." Janice shrugged. "You've changed since you went inside. Not sure we're really suited any more."

"Well, thanks a bunch." Brian knocked his chair over with a crash and put his face up close to hers. "You can just piss off, then. You and your fancy family and fancy food." He left the room, slamming the door behind him, and they heard him go out the front and down the drive.

"Is it nice to be home, Livvy?" Sue carried on eating.

"Yes, thank you, Mum. It just got a bit better, too."

Janice glanced up. "Sorry, sis. He was a loser."

"Well, I think we all knew that, Jan. Glad you finally realised. Where has he gone, then? Back to yours?"

Janice shook her head. "No, he still has his own place. Well, it's his Mum's, really, I guess, but he dosses there a bit. On that estate round the corner from me."

"Well, I'm very glad he's gone. Not one of your better choices."

Olivia wiped her garlic bread around her plate to mop up the last of the chilli, and her heart did a little flip as she imagined herself out on a date with Adam. She wouldn't be able to wipe her plate with her bread at the Ritz. He'd probably be appalled at her table manners.

She laid down her fork and glanced around the table. Her parents and aunt were all still eating, her aunt shovelling in her chilli like there was no tomorrow, her long, rather greasy ponytail swinging round and almost brushing her plate. Oh, God, her family were so different to Adam's. Maybe he wouldn't even want to go out with her. Always assuming he ever came back.

Her heart plummeted as she remembered he had no easy way to contact her, and she wanted nothing more than to scurry up to her room, crawl into bed, and cry herself to sleep. It had all been such fun at the cottage. It had been fun fooling her friends, fun practising, and even more fun when the practising became for real. But now—now it wasn't fun at all. The arrival of Naomi had cast a black pall over everything, and however much Adam, or her mother, assured her the girl had been lying, there was a part of her that didn't believe that. And with each hour that passed, that part was getting bigger.

"Are you okay, love?"

Olivia glanced up to find her mother watching her. She shrugged. "No. Not really. But there's nothing I can do about it."

"What's the problem?" Janice looked up and wiped her mouth with the back of her hand. "You got boyfriend trouble too?"

"Maybe."

"Olivia met someone when she was away," Sue told her sister. "She's rather fond of him, but he has to sort something out before they can be together. I think she's worrying needlessly."

"Another woman, is it?" Janice looked sympathetic. "We've all been there."

"No. It's not like that." Olivia pushed back her chair and stood up. "Mum, I don't want any pudding. I think I'll just go to bed."

"Okay. You go on, and Livvy, don't worry. It'll all work out fine."

"I hope you're right. Night, Dad. Night, Janice. Glad you ditched Brian. He was well creepy. You can do better than that." She turned and left the room and headed upstairs to her bedroom.

Although she had left home nearly four years ago, her bedroom still looked the same as it had since she was about fifteen. A white painted bookcase was against one wall, crammed with books dating right back to her early childhood. The wardrobe still contained a lot of her old clothes that she hadn't wanted to take with her when she moved out, and her mother had found it easier just to leave them there. The single bed was pushed against the far wall, alongside the window that looked out over the garden.

Olivia sat down on the edge of the bed and sighed. She really felt like her life was just one big mess. First the break up with Chris, albeit not really a trauma, more of a relief; then the weird few days playacting in Devon with Adam. And now what?

What was actually going to happen next? Was he really going to arrive on the doorstep and sweep her off in a limo to the Ritz? It was hardly likely. If he found her at all it would be a miracle. And suppose Naomi had been telling the truth? She still didn't trust that he wouldn't feel he was honour bound to stay with her.

With a groan, Olivia fell backwards onto the bed and covered her face with her hands. Why couldn't she be like Sarah and Jon and be in a normal, boring, stable relationship? She rolled onto her stomach and buried her face in the pillow. Because then she wouldn't have had Adam. And if she was honest, even the couple of days they'd had together were worth more than several years of a boring, ordinary relationship.

She wriggled off the bed, pulled off her socks, and slid in under the quilt, pulling it up to her chin. She reached over and turned off the bedside light and lay staring up at the ceiling. The light from the moon was sneaking in through the gap in the curtain and casting a shadow across her face.

Maybe Adam would turn up tomorrow. Tuesday, Jess had said. She reckoned he would have sorted it all out by Tuesday. It was Tuesday tomorrow.

Chapter 12

Tuesday 29th December

"Liv, aren't you going to get dressed, pet?" Sue's head poked around the door of the living room. "It's nearly midday."

"What's the point?" Olivia looked up from the sofa and shrugged. "I'm not going anywhere."

"And suppose your young man turns up? What's he going to think, finding you in your pyjamas, with your hair looking like a haystack?"

"He's not coming."

"He might. Now, come on, get yourself tidied up. You're making the place look a mess."

"Mum! Honestly, you don't care about me, just about how tidy the house is." Olivia got to her feet with a reluctant grin. "Okay, I'll get dressed, but I really don't see why I have to. I'm only going to stay here and watch TV."

She trudged up the stairs and went into her bedroom with a sigh. Pulling her pyjamas off, she left them in a heap on the floor and then searched around for something to wear. Eventually she pulled on her jeans, a long baggy jumper, and a pair of red fluffy socks.

That would have to do. If Adam did turn up, at least she was decent.

177

The further through Tuesday it got, the more unlikely she felt his arrival would be. Although if she thought about it logically, it *was* only two days since he'd gone off with Naomi. Maybe that wasn't long enough to sort it out. And then to track her down. Yeah, he did have a lot to do. Maybe she shouldn't be giving up hope yet.

Back in the living room, she curled up on the sofa again and flicked on the TV. Her father had gone back to work, and her mother was currently doing something in the kitchen, so she had it to herself for the time being. She scrolled through the channels and finally decided on a re-run of *Friends*. So long as it wasn't an episode where they were having relationship problems, it ought to cheer her up.

It had just reached the adverts when her mobile bleeped. It was a text from Jess.

"Coming over after work to take you out. Have a think where you'd like to go."

Olivia sighed and sent a reply: *"Not in the mood. I'd be rotten company."*

"Tough. I'm coming anyway. Be there about six. Make sure you're dressed."

She rolled her eyes but couldn't help a small smile. Jess could be very bossy. She texted back. *"You're bossy. Okay, I guess. Somewhere local."*

She put the phone on the coffee table and finished watching the episode of *Friends*, realising as it ended that she hadn't been paying attention at all and had no idea what it had been about.

"Would you like some lunch?" Sue's head appeared around the door. "I'm having some cheese on toast."

Olivia stretched and shrugged. "I s'pose so. Thanks. Jess wants me to go out with her tonight."

"Do you good." Sue disappeared again, her voice floating back from the kitchen. "You need something to take your mind off this situation."

With a sigh, Olivia got to her feet and wandered into the kitchen to join her. "Maybe. Just don't feel like being sociable."

"Unless it's with Adam."

"Of course." She leaned against the worktop and folded her arms. "And the more time that goes by the less I think that's likely to happen. Oh, Mum, he's really nice. Why has this happened?"

"Don't be so negative." Sue put the cheese on toast under the grill. "It's only been two days. I imagine it could take a lot longer than that for him to sort it out. And then he has to find you. It would have been much easier, of course, if you'd remembered to exchange phone numbers, but you didn't, so nothing we can do about that." She glanced over at Olivia. "But it's really no good moping around here all the time. He'll find you and it'll all work out. I'm absolutely sure of it."

"Mum, you're basing that on romantic novels and films, you know you are. And they don't always have happy endings."

"The ones I read and watch do."

"Rubbish." Olivia shook her head. "You're obsessed by *Love Actually*. That didn't work out for all of them."

"Don't be pedantic." Sue grinned at her. "You know what I mean. From what you've said about this Adam, he sounds like a real gentleman. He won't let you down."

"That's part of the problem." Olivia put her hands up to cover her face. "I think he may be so much of a gentleman that he thinks he has to marry her."

"She's not pregnant." Sue rescued the toast from under the grill. "Oldest trick in the book. Trust me, she's not pregnant." She held out a plate to Olivia. "Here you go. Let's take them in the living room and watch TV while we eat. When are you meeting Jess?"

"She's coming over at six." Olivia followed her mother and slumped down on the sofa again. "But I really don't want to go out. I just want to go to bed."

"Liv, this really isn't like you to be so negative." Sue watched her in concern. "You've had boy problems before."

"This is different."

"Do you love him?"

"Don't be ridiculous. I've only known him for a couple of days." Olivia felt her face getting hot and looked down at her plate.

"So? You can fall in love at first sight. Did you sleep with him?"

"Mum! I already told you, we slept in the same bed but we didn't have sex."

"Did you do anything?"

"No. No. Not really."

"What's that supposed to mean?"

"Nothing."

"Livvy, I want to help you. It would be easier if you actually told me stuff."

"We kissed. I already told you that too."

"And?"

Olivia put her plate on the coffee table and sighed. "We had to cuddle to keep warm. And then…"

"And then?" Sue prompted, watching her closely.

"He did something."

"God, Livvy, this is like pulling teeth! What did he do? You can tell me anything, you know that. I *have* read *Fifty Shades*."

"Dear god, Mother! It was nothing like that! What are you like?" Olivia stared at her mother in horror. "He just did this thing to my neck which…was…really nice."

"Ah, he found an erogenous zone and gave you an orgasm." Sue sat back, a look of satisfaction on her face. "Why didn't you just say that?"

"Because you're my mother! This is not a normal conversation." Olivia started to giggle and lay back on the cushions. "Honestly no one else talks to their mother like this."

"Well, you're very lucky, then," Sue said with a smug smile.

"I suppose so." Olivia grinned back at her. "It just seems weird. But god, Mum, it was amazing! But we didn't have proper sex."

"Why?"

"He said he wanted to get Naomi out of his life first, and then he could be mine properly."

"Hmmmm, he does seem like a gentleman." Sue put her head on one side. "Not a perfect gentleman, perhaps, or you wouldn't have done anything, but it's quite nice that he wanted to wait."

"I guess. Would have been nice, though."

"Well, you still have that to look forward to now. So are you in love with him?"

"I told you it's too soon for that."

"No, it's not, and I think you are. You wouldn't be

this upset about it all if he was just a potential good shag."

"Mum, really? You're supposed to set a good example to me!"

"What am I doing wrong? I think you're in love with him, and that's a nice thing. I can't wait to meet him. Remind me what he looks like again."

"He's six foot one... He told me that. I didn't measure him. He has dark chestnut hair. It looks quite red in some lights, and he has really piercing green eyes." Olivia curled up in the corner of the sofa and smiled. "He is quite honestly the best-looking man I've ever seen. Even with a big black bruise on his forehead."

"Oh, that often makes them even more attractive." Sue nodded enthusiastically. "Makes them seem vulnerable and in need of rescuing. That's very sexy. He does sound lovely."

"He is." Olivia cuddled a cushion tightly. "D'you really think it'll all turn out okay?"

"Of course it will." Sue spoke with confidence. "You'll see. Now, let's watch a soppy film for the afternoon, and then you can get ready to go out with Jess. You should go and have a good old natter to take your mind off things."

****

"Where are we going, then?" Olivia followed Jess down the path and out to her car.

"How about the Green Man? They have good music on the juke box."

"Meh. I guess. I used to go there with Chris sometimes. It's a bit of a dive."

"Come on, it'll be a laugh." Jess unlocked the car

and they got in. "I can't stay out too late, got to be at work for eight tomorrow."

Olivia pulled her seatbelt across her and did it up. "Okay, then. They have quite nice wine there, actually. Oh, you won't be able to drink, though."

"It's all right." Jess shrugged. "Next time we go out you can drive." She set off down the street and turned out onto the main road. "So how are you doing?"

"Badly." Olivia slumped down in her seat. "It's Tuesday evening, Jess. He hasn't called or turned up yet."

"Well, that is only two days. Give it time." Jess indicated to turn left and headed for the large pub at the end of the road. "Have you told your mum about him? What does she say?"

"Oh, god, I had the most weird conversation with her this afternoon!" Olivia rolled her eyes and laughed. "I ended up telling her about the neck thing."

"God, Livvy! You told your mum? Why?"

"Well, you know what she's like. She was imagining all sorts of *Fifty Shades* things going on, so I had to tell her what actually happened."

"Why on earth would she have thought that?" Jess stared at her in amazement as she parked the car and turned off the engine. "How on earth did you even get onto the subject of sex?"

"Well she asked me if we'd done it."

"And she didn't take no for an answer?" Jess locked the car doors, and they moved towards the pub entrance.

"Well, I guess I was a bit hesitant, so she could tell we did something. And she kept asking if I was in love with him."

"And are you?"

"Oh, not you too!" Olivia sighed and pushed open the door. "I've only known him for a couple of days. It's way too soon."

"So why are you so upset about it all, then?" Jess was looking around for a table. "I think you're in love with him. You told me you thought he might be the one."

"Might be."

"Look, there's a table over there. You go and grab it, and I'll get the drinks in. D'you want any crisps or anything?"

Olivia shook her head and wove her way through the crowds towards the small table in the corner, beside the fruit machine. She squeezed behind it and sat down, wriggling out of her jacket at the same time. Glancing around, she recognised quite a few of the young men who were standing at the bar, friends of Chris. Her heart plummeted as she realised she could very well bump into him. That would be awkward.

"Here we go." Jess appeared, put the drinks on the slightly sticky table, and slid into the seat opposite to Olivia. "Busy tonight, for a Tuesday."

"Still Christmas holidays for a lot of people, me included. Guess they're making the most of it." Olivia took a sip of wine. "Thanks. Cheers."

"Cheers." Jess raised her lime and soda. "Did you say you used to come here with Chris?"

"Yeah. There's some of his mates over at the bar. Hope he doesn't show up."

Jess twisted round to view the men and wrinkled her nose. "Typical football types," she said dismissively. "Was Chris like that, then? The real

Chris," she added with a grin.

"Yep. Mad about football and drinking with the lads. Not quite sure why he used to bring me along, actually. He more or less ignored me once his friends arrived."

"Be funny if he turned up." Jess grinned as she took a drink. "Think he'd speak to you?"

"Probably." Olivia felt quite depressed at the prospect. "Now I've met Adam, I keep wondering what on earth I was doing even going out with Chris."

"If he came in, would you tell him about Adam?"

"What would be the point?" Olivia shrugged. "I don't really want to talk to him. Now let's talk about something else. What did you say you and Tom are doing at New Year's?"

"Just going to the pub down the road from my Mum's. They always have a good party there. Saves going too far, and we can stay with them and walk home."

"Is that the Red Dragon? I remember going there when we were about sixteen."

"Yeah. Bit of a dive, but they always do a good party. Mum and Dad like it."

"Oh, shit." Olivia slid down in her seat and held her glass in front of her face. "Chris has just walked in."

"Ooh, where?" Jess twisted round again, her eyes eagerly scanning the room. "Is that him?"

Olivia peeped over her glass and nodded. "Yeah."

"Okay. Doesn't really look your type. But you did say you were desperate."

"God, Jess, what a way to put it. I just said I hadn't had a date in a while, so when he asked, I said yes. I wasn't desperate. I've never been desperate." She sneaked a look across the room to where Chris had joined his friends at the bar. He was wearing rather baggy jeans which hung a little too low, a navy blue T-shirt, and a brown leather jacket. He'd had his hair cut since Olivia had seen him last, and she was horrified to see just how short he'd had it done. "Oh, I hope he doesn't see me."

"Too late." Jess grinned at her. "Look, one of his friends must have clocked you when we came in. He's pointing you out to him."

Olivia sank even further down in her seat. "Oh, shit. And here he comes. Great."

"Liv. Fancy seeing you here." Chris approached their table, slopping a little beer over the edge of his glass as he squeezed his way through the crowds. "What happened to you, then? You disappeared after that party."

Olivia stared at him in disbelief. "What?"

"I thought we were going to some cottage or other for Christmas. But you just left."

"Is your brain completely addled with that stuff?" Olivia nodded towards the pint in his hand. "We broke up, remember? I found you mauling some woman in the kitchen."

"Did you?" Chris scratched his head. "God, that evening's a bit of a blur, to be honest. You must be Jess. Liv told me all about you."

"Chris, what do you want?" Olivia snapped, her patience wearing thin.

"Just to see what happened to you."

"Yet you didn't think to call me, or text me, to find out?"

"Nah, well, I thought something was up between us, just couldn't remember what, so I thought I'd let you cool off over Christmas and see you after."

"Well, you're right, something was up between us. We broke up. End of. Now go away and leave me alone." Olivia took a long drink of her wine and glared at him.

"So I can't just apologise for whatever it was, then?"

"You snogged another woman!" Olivia ground her teeth in frustration. "No, you can't apologise. We have broken up. We broke up nearly a week ago. I can't believe you don't remember."

Chris shrugged. "It does ring a bell now, actually. So that's it, then, is it? We're not going out anymore?"

"You've got it. We're not going out anymore, or ever will be again. Now, goodbye, Chris."

With another shrug, he took a long slurp of beer, winked at Jess, and then turned and wended his way back to his friends at the bar.

Olivia put her elbows on the table and rested her head in her hands. "I am so embarrassed," she muttered. "How could I ever have considered taking him down to the cottage for Christmas? Imagine what Sarah would have said."

"Yes." Jess was watching his rather laborious progress across the room. "I think you had a lucky escape there. What were you thinking, Livvy? I reckon he was your worst choice yet. I thought you said he was not bad-looking."

"Well, I thought he was okay at the time. He's had his hair cut since last week. It used to look a lot better than that. And he can look smart—he was wearing a suit when I first met him, actually, but I think you're right. I must have been desperate. Sorry about that."

"Don't be daft." Jess turned back to her. "We all make mistakes. Everyone has an ex they want to forget about."

"Aunt Janice has dozens." Olivia grinned. "She broke up with Brian in the middle of dinner last night. God, he was really awful."

"I bet Adam seems a world away from this, doesn't he?" Jess took a sip of her drink.

"So much so it doesn't even seem real any more." Olivia sighed. "Did it really happen? Will he come back, Jess? Do you really think he will?"

"Of course he will. Anyone could see he was nuts about you. Even Sarah picked up on that. He'll be back for you. Just give him time to sort out that woman."

"And you reckon he'll find me?"

"Of course he will. He knows your name and roughly where you live. He'll find you. May not be till after New Year's, though. D'you want to come out with me and Tom?"

Olivia shook her head. "No, thanks. I'll just stay at Mum and Dad's. Not really in the mood for partying."

"Well, you may still find you're going to the Ritz, or was that a joke?"

"No. It wasn't a joke, but I'm not going to hold my breath. I have nothing to wear for that anyway." Olivia grinned at Jess. "You know, he asked if he needed a tux for Christmas Day."

"What?"

"Yeah, we went shopping at a local supermarket on Christmas Eve because he didn't have any clothes with him—obviously—and he bought all sorts of stuff.

Asked if we dressed up for dinner and would he need a tux. I told him pyjamas would be more appropriate."

"Do supermarkets sell tuxedos, then?" Jess was grinning widely.

"No, that's what he was worried about. I do worry we might be a bit too different, though."

"You'll be fine. All that matters is you like each other." Jess took a sip of her drink and watched Olivia over the rim. "Or love each other, even."

"Stop saying that." Olivia wriggled in her seat. "I told you it's too soon for that."

"Why are you refusing to admit it? It's obvious to me—and your mum, by the sound of it."

Olivia was silent for a moment. "Because he might not come back. He might stay with Naomi."

"And if he does, it's not going to make it any easier just because you didn't admit you loved him." Jess leant forward and took her hand. "Not that he will stay with her, so you may as well tell me."

"I don't know." Olivia sighed. "Maybe it's just lust. I really, really want to have sex with him. Maybe it's just that. He's so hot."

"I reckon it's more than that. You seem to get on so well."

"We do. We have the same sense of humour, and it's just nice being with him." Olivia grimaced. "That's why it's so hard waiting to see what happens."

"Yeah." Jess nodded. "You're definitely in love. It's not just sex. Now, d'you want another drink?"

"Yeah, another wine'd be great, but I'll get these. You bought the first round." She started to get to her feet.

"Chris is still there." Jess stood up. "Give me the

money, and I'll go."

Olivia glanced over at the bar, where Chris was standing with a group of his friends, all laughing loudly at something. As she watched, he downed his pint and caught the attention of the barmaid for a refill.

"What was I thinking?" she muttered, sitting down again. "Honestly, Jess, I'm sure he wasn't such a Neanderthal last week."

Jess chuckled. "You're just comparing him to perfect Adam. He's bound to come up wanting. D'you want crisps this time?"

"Yeah, cheese and onion, please." Olivia fished in her bag and pulled out a twenty-pound note. "And a bar of chocolate." She kept watching Chris as he appeared to be indulging in a drinking race with two of his friends, and shuddered as she realised she'd had a relationship with him. Never again would she be tempted to go out with someone just because they asked.

She sat back in her chair and closed her eyes. Hopefully she wouldn't be in that situation again. If everything turned out as it should.

Chapter 13

New Year's Eve

"Want some tea, Livvy?" Sue called from the kitchen.

Olivia curled up even more into the corner of the sofa and cuddled a cushion tightly. "No, thanks." She stared at the TV screen blankly, not taking in what was on it, her mind miles away. Wednesday had come and gone with no word from Adam, and it was now Thursday afternoon. It was New Year's Eve, and she still hadn't heard from him. With each hour that passed, she was slipping further and further into a pit of despair.

She jumped as her phone bleeped, and she reached out to pick it up. Jess. She sighed and opened the message.

"Are you all right? Have you got dressed today?"

With a grunt of annoyance, Olivia wrote a reply. *"No. How d'you know I'm not dressed?"*

"Your mum told me."

Olivia scowled at the phone. "Mum! Have you been talking to Jess?"

Sue appeared in the doorway, mug in hand. "Why?" she asked cautiously, walking over and sitting down at the other end of the sofa.

"She says you told her I haven't got dressed. What

the hell?"

"Well, I may have texted her." Sue looked awkward. "I was worried about you. You haven't got dressed for two days, Liv. It's not healthy. And suppose Adam turns up? Have you looked in the mirror today?"

"He's not going to turn up, Mum." Olivia hugged the cushion more tightly. "It's been four days now. Plenty of time to sort things out. He's going to stay with her, I know he is. And I'll have to go out with some other loser like Chris."

"Good god, Livvy, don't be ridiculous! Four days still isn't long, and why on earth does that mean you have to go out with a loser again?" Sue leaned forward and brushed Olivia's tangled hair off her face. "I only told Jess because I thought she might be able to cheer you up. You should go out with her and Tom tonight."

"I don't want to." Olivia pulled back from her mother in annoyance. "Look at me. I wouldn't be very good company, would I? No, I'll just stay here with you and Dad. Janice isn't coming over, is she?"

"No." Sue shook her head. "Actually, your dad and I were thinking of going down the King's Head for a couple of pints. You could come with us, if you like."

"Oh, right." Olivia looked even more miserable. "So I'll be here alone, then? Great New Year."

"Right. That's it." Sue got to her feet. "You have to snap out of this. You have two invitations to go out, and you're going to choose to stay here alone and feel sorry for yourself. Come on, Livvy, go and have a shower and get dressed. You'll feel much better."

"No." Olivia shook her head obstinately. "I don't want to feel better. Until Adam comes back, I won't feel better, and he's not coming."

"Of course he is." Sue sat down again. "Give him time, sweetie. I promise you he'll be back. That girl wasn't pregnant, you can rely on that. But it may take him a while to get her to admit it. Please at least go and have a wash."

"Why, do I smell? Am I offending you?"

"No, of course not. But you will feel better. And I'll make pizza for supper if you like. Your favourite."

"Have you got anchovies?"

"I have."

"Olives?"

"Black and green."

"All right, then. I'd like that. But I'm not getting washed or dressed."

Sue patted her hand and stood up. "Okay, then. Would you mind if we went out for a bit later? Would you be all right on your own?"

Olivia shrugged. "I guess. Yeah, you go and enjoy yourselves. No point in me making you miserable as well." She picked up the remote control and began to flick through the TV channels, uncomfortably aware that her mother was still watching her. Glancing out of the corner of her eye, she saw her shake her head and then disappear in the direction of the kitchen.

Olivia sighed and gave up looking for something to watch. Nothing was grabbing her attention, and she was much happier just being miserable and feeling sorry for herself. She wriggled down until she was lying flat out on the sofa, the cushion still clutched firmly to her chest.

Why did everyone keep telling her to cheer up and saying that Adam would come back? Of course he wouldn't. By now he was probably all cosily engaged to Naomi and busy planning the nursery.

She rolled onto her side and screwed her eyes shut. What an amazing thought it would be if *she* was having his baby. It would be the most beautiful baby in the world, and they would be the most wonderful parents. That bitch didn't deserve him. How could he forgive her?

She sat up and pushed her hair out of her eyes. Why was she so sure he had? Why was she so sure he wasn't coming back? There could only really be one reason. She really was in love with him and consequently couldn't help imagining all the worst possible scenarios. Maybe her mum was right. Maybe it was just taking him longer than he thought. She pulled her knees up to her chin. But she still wasn't getting dressed or going out.

****

"Is the pizza nearly ready?" Olivia wandered into the kitchen and leant up against the worktop. "I'm actually getting hungry now."

"Soon." Sue wiped a strand of hair back from her face. "Glad you're getting your appetite back. It's only six fifteen. It'll be about half an hour. Where's your dad?"

"He's watching telly. Are you still going out later?"

"Would you rather we didn't?" Sue glanced over at her. "We can stay home and play games if you like."

"No." Olivia shook her head, a lump forming in her throat. "We played games in the cottage at Christmas."

"Well, we could play different games. We'll do whatever you want. It's a pity Claire's working again. It might have cheered you up to have her over."

"Not really." Olivia shrugged. "She has a boyfriend she never stops talking about. Still, at least Janice isn't coming."

"No, she's going out with some girlfriends. Probably to pick up some other lowlife like Brian again. God, I wish she'd be a bit more choosy. She's over forty now. Time she settled down a bit."

"That'll never happen." Olivia managed a grin. "Can you imagine Janice with a baby?"

Sue rolled her eyes. "I cannot. What a dreadful thought! Not a nice thing to say about my own sister, but she would be a terrible mother." She smiled at Olivia. "You, on the other hand, would be a great mum."

"I hope so." Olivia shrugged. "Wish it was me that was pregnant, not Naomi."

"Well, it's a bit soon for that." Sue grinned. "But I get what you mean. But remember, Naomi's not pregnant. Trust me."

"Where is he, then?" Without waiting for a reply, Olivia turned and went back into the living room, flopping down on the sofa and staring at the TV. "What you watching?"

"Nothing much." Paul smiled at her. "Just channel hopping. Honestly, we pay for all these channels, and there's never anything on I want to watch. Waste of money. Aren't you going to go out tonight, then, love? With Jess, maybe?"

"No. Why does everyone keep trying to make me go out? Are you wanting to get rid of me?" Olivia scowled and punched a cushion.

"No, of course not. Just thought it might cheer you up a bit. Your mum and I might go down the King's

Head later. You're welcome to come with us."

"Mum said. No, thanks, I'll just stay here."

"Maybe you should get dressed. Might buck you up a bit."

"Oh, god, not you too. Mum, Jess, and you. Why can't you all leave me alone?" She curled her legs up under her and wriggled back into the cushions.

A sudden buzz from the doorbell made them both look up, and Paul started to get up.

"I'll get it." Sue's voice carried through as she went towards the front door and pulled it open. After a moment, Olivia could hear the murmur of voices, and then her mother laughed. "Oh, come in, come in. Livvy, someone to see you."

The living room door opened, and Sue stood aside to let the visitor in, a huge grin on her face. Olivia held her breath as Adam appeared behind her mother and hovered uncertainly in the doorway. He was wearing a tux and looked even more gorgeous than he had the last time she saw him. His hair was deliciously dishevelled and flopping across his forehead, which still sported a now yellowing bruise. He smiled at her.

"Hello."

"Hello." She scrambled to her feet, still clutching the cushion, and stared at him, suddenly dreadfully aware of how she looked.

"I found you, then."

"Yes."

"I told you he would." Sue was grinning in delight, her eyes roving all over Adam's body. "You were quite right, too."

"Mum!" Olivia's voice was strangled. "I'm not dressed. I'm sorry."

Adam grinned. "It's okay. You still look lovely. But you may want to put something else on. The Ritz does have a dress code."

"What?"

"The Ritz. Our date. Remember?"

"We're still going?"

"Well, I am. I was rather hoping you'd be there too. Not much of a date if you're not."

"How did you find me? We forgot to exchange phone numbers."

"I know. That was very silly of us. You weren't all that hard to track down."

"I told you he'd manage it." Sue nodded to Adam. "What did you do, then? Track her on the computer?"

Adam grinned. "Well, I knew your surname, and Olivia had said you lived in a semi in Romford. First I checked the phone book for all the Marshalls in Romford, and then I used online maps to find which of the houses were semi-detached. Then I just made a list so I could go to them all until I found her. This is the fourth house I've been to."

"Oh, that's so romantic!" Sue clapped her hands. "Just like when Hugh Grant goes looking for Martine McCutcheon at the end of *Love Actually*!" She peered towards the door. "Do you have a chauffeur-driven limo, as well?"

Adam looked slightly embarrassed. "Well, yes, actually. I thought it would be nice for our first date."

"Livvy, come and get dressed." Sue held out her hand to Olivia. "Paul, get Adam a drink. We won't be long."

"Don't rush. The table's not booked until eight thirty." Adam smiled. "I didn't know how long it would take to find you."

"Why didn't you phone?" Olivia was staring at him. "You must have had the phone numbers of all the people."

"I did." Adam smiled down at her. "I thought this would be more romantic. And I was worried you'd say no on the phone. This way you don't have any choice."

"I wouldn't have said no." She stared up at him, her stomach turning somersaults. "But is everything all right?"

"I'll tell you everything later." He grinned. "Right now, I think you might need to go and get ready. Your hair looks like a haystack again."

Olivia felt her face flush and allowed her mother to pull her out of the room and usher her upstairs.

"Mum, slow down. I don't have anything to wear. All my posh dresses are at the flat. What am I going to do?"

Sue pushed her into the bedroom and went over to the wardrobe. "I've already thought of that. I still have your prom dress here. And Claire's. One of those should do for the Ritz."

"My prom dress? Mum that's nearly eight years old! It won't fit."

"Of course it'll fit. You haven't put on an ounce of weight since school. Look, here it is." Sue pulled it out of the wardrobe and laid it on the bed. "I think that would be okay for a posh dinner."

Olivia stared down at the dress. It was electric blue, with a tight strapless top and a long floaty skirt covered in a layer of chiffon and finished off with a satin sash. She picked it up and held it against her. "I guess it might do. I did look nice in it."

"You looked lovely, and you'll look even better tonight." Sue took it off her. "I'll just check it over, in case it needs a stitch anywhere, while you go and shower."

Olivia stared at her. "Mum. He came. He's actually here."

"I told you he would. Always trust your mother." Sue looked smug. "And he is totally gorgeous. You were right about that. Those eyes are amazing."

"Mum, hands off…you've got Dad! Adam is mine. It's not like my clothes. You can't borrow him."

"I can look." Sue grinned cheekily. "That's all. Now go and shower."

Olivia went into the bathroom and peeled off her rather stale pyjamas. She glanced at herself in the mirror and groaned. Her hair, usually very flat and sleek, was knotted and standing on end. It was going to take quite a bit to sort that out.

She turned on the shower and hopped in, standing directly underneath and letting the hot water run all over her. Adam had really come for her. He was really taking her to the Ritz. It was almost unbelievable. She stuck her head under the water and screwed her eyes shut.

But had he sorted it all out with Naomi? Did it mean he was free to be hers? She poured the shampoo onto her head and rubbed vigorously. He looked so gorgeous in the tux, too. Just like she imagined he would. And he wanted to take her out. In a limo, to the Ritz.

She finished washing, shaved her armpits and legs, and got out of the shower, pulling a towel off the heated rail and wrapping it around her. She grabbed another one and rubbed her hair with it. She wasn't really going to have time to do anything fancy with it. Just dry it and wear it loose would probably be best.

She tossed the towels back onto the rail and went through into the bedroom. Her mother was busy packing a small overnight bag.

"Mum? What's that for? We're going out for dinner."

"You never know. I wouldn't be surprised if he booked a room at the Ritz, too. Just being prepared." Sue smiled at her. "Your dress is fine. Now get your hair dried, and we can sort out your makeup."

"Mum, I can't take an overnight bag! I mustn't presume."

"No, I've just packed it as a precaution. Then it'll be ready if he says you need it. Come on, dry that hair before you put your dress on."

With a giggle, Olivia picked up her hairbrush and smoothed the tangles out of her hair. "Mum, you think of everything. I suppose you got that idea from a book, did you?"

"Of course. My reading comes in handy sometimes. Here, let me dry your hair." She picked up the hairdryer and directed it at Olivia's head, taking the brush from her and smoothing the hair as she went. "Your hair dries very quickly. This shouldn't take long. Good job you don't need to straighten it."

Fifteen minutes later, Olivia was breathing in while Sue zipped her into her dress. Her long hair was hanging glossy and silky over her shoulders, and her makeup looked as near perfect as she could get it.

"There, how does that feel? Is it too tight?"

"I can cope." Olivia nodded. "I just won't eat too

much! Too excited to eat, actually." She stepped forward and looked at herself in the mirror. "Oh, that looks nice. I'd forgotten how pretty it is." She twirled around and laughed. "This is fun. I'm so glad you kept the dresses."

"Well, I thought they might come in handy one day." Sue looked pleased with herself. "Ready, then? Shall we go downstairs and wow him?"

"Shoes!" Olivia stopped and stared at her in horror. "I don't have any shoes! I only have my Converse and my boots. What am I going to do?"

"No worries." Sue disappeared in the direction of her bedroom. "I have just the thing." A moment later she reappeared with a pair of very high heels the exact colour of the dress. "These will be perfect."

Olivia stared at the shoes. "Mum, those are mine. How long have you had them? I wondered where they'd gone."

"Ooh, a couple of months. You left them here one weekend. They look really good with skinny jeans and my blue top."

"*My* blue top." Olivia grinned. "Mum, I despair of you, but on this occasion it's worked out well. Yeah, these shoes look awesome." She spun round. "So do I really look okay?"

"You look beautiful. Really beautiful." Sue moved over and gave her a hug. "Now, come on, we've been nearly forty-five minutes. Goodness knows what they're talking about down there."

Olivia left the room and started down the stairs, carefully holding her dress up with one hand. Her heart was pounding wildly as she got to the bottom and stepped into the living room. Adam was sitting on the sofa, clutching a glass of what looked to be wine, listening politely while Paul regaled him with some longwinded story about the relationship between postmen and dogs. They both looked up as Olivia entered, and there was a stunned silence.

"You look very nice, love." Paul smiled at his daughter.

Olivia looked over at Adam. He slowly got to his feet and walked a few steps closer to her.

"You look absolutely stunning." His voice shook slightly. "I have never seen anyone more beautiful."

"Thank you," Olivia whispered. "This is just an old dress…"

"Shhh." Adam held up his hand. "Just accept the compliment. You are gorgeous." He took another step forward and took hold of her hand. "Are you ready to go?"

She nodded, not trusting herself to speak.

"Have a lovely time, pet." Paul smiled at them. "And think of us down the King's Head."

"Paul, really! Okay, darling, have you got everything you need?" Sue raised her eyebrows hopefully.

"Oh, I should have said." Adam glanced at her. "I've booked a room for tonight. If you don't mind me keeping her out…?"

"She's a grown woman. She can do what she likes." Sue smiled at him. "So she'll need this, then?" She produced the overnight bag from just outside the door and held it out.

Adam took it with a grin. "Yes, she will. How very perceptive of you."

Olivia felt her face begin to get hot, and looked

away in confusion. "Mum, stop embarrassing me. She packed that, not me."

Adam chuckled and put his arm around her shoulders. "Stop worrying. Your mother is just trying to help. It's nice to see she approves of me enough for that."

"Well, if you'd heard the things she's been saying about you the last few days..." Sue grinned and leaned forward to give Olivia a kiss on the cheek. "Now, go on. Go and have fun, and I want to hear all about the Ritz."

"Oh, my phone, I don't have my phone." Olivia scooped it up from the arm of the sofa and popped it into her bag. "Okay, I'm ready."

Adam took her hand and walked to the door. "Very nice to meet you." He smiled back at her parents. "I look forward to getting to know you better. I'll take good care of her." He ushered her down the path towards the waiting limo that was attracting rather a lot of attention from the neighbours.

Silently Olivia climbed into the back and arranged her dress carefully. Her heart was beating almost uncontrollably, and she was feeling a little short of breath. She could hardly believe this was actually happening. She had spent so much time the last few days resigning herself to him not coming back that it was really hard to get her head around. Adam got in beside her, and the car moved smoothly off along the road, watched by several open-mouthed bystanders that Olivia tried hard to avoid looking at.

"Hello." Adam's hand reached over and took hers.

"Hello." She glanced up at him. "I didn't think you were coming back. These last few days have been awful."

"I told you I'd come back for you. You should have trusted me. The only problem was not knowing where you were."

"But Naomi… You might have stayed with her."

"No. I told you that was never going to happen."

"But I thought…" Olivia looked down at his hand holding hers. "I thought if she was pregnant you might feel you had to marry her, or something."

He put his finger under her chin and made her look up at him. "I wasn't going to go back to her, whatever the situation." He held her gaze. "I did tell you that. I don't love her. I want to be with you."

"So was she pregnant?" Olivia wasn't even sure she wanted to hear the answer.

"No. I was sure it was a lie, and I was right." He sighed. "Unfortunately, it took me three days to get the truth out of her. In fact, she never did tell me. James did."

"Your best friend?"

"Ex-best friend. Yeah. He found out what she was doing and told me. She got the test from a friend."

"So what happened?"

"Do you really want to know? Won't it spoil the evening?"

"No." Olivia shook her head. "I want to get it all out the way now. Before our date."

"Okay. Fair enough. James told me what he knew, and I confronted her with it. At first she denied it and insisted she was pregnant, but I told her I knew which friend she had got the test from, and that James knew what she was up to. So eventually she admitted she wasn't, but kept insisting she loved me and wanted me to forgive her. I told her she had a very funny way of showing her love." He paused for a moment and ran a hand through his hair. "It wasn't a very nice few days. And all the time I was worrying about you. I didn't realise about the phone numbers until I'd been back home for several hours. I'd failed to get her to admit anything and thought I'd just text you to see if you were okay, when I realised I couldn't." He glanced at her. "That was a dreadful moment, actually, because I could imagine how you were feeling and I wasn't even able to speak to you."

"Did you tell her about me?" Olivia forced the words out.

"Not at first. I was too busy trying to trip her up in her story. But she did ask why I was at the cottage, of course, so in the end I did tell her about you." He grinned. "I said you found me on the beach and kidnapped me."

"Adam! You didn't!" Olivia's hand shot up to cover her mouth.

"Not really." He chuckled. "I told her you found me on the beach and looked after me. And yes, she probably hates you, although I did explain that she'd already blown it with me before I ever met you."

"So she's going to stalk me now and put horses' heads in my bed, is she?"

"Hopefully not. Not horses' heads, anyway. She likes horses. Possibly a fox or two." He grinned at her. "I honestly had a few moments over the last few days when I wished I really could kill her and bury her in the garden. It would have made things so much easier."

"I guess it would." Olivia looked up at him. "She won't really stalk me, will she?"

"Of course not. She's not a psycho. I rather suspect she and James might get together, actually. I never did believe it was a one-off."

"He'd get together with her even though she was trying to trick you into staying with her?" Olivia stared at him.

"He's weak." Adam shrugged. "Always was, and always wanted what I had. It's not the first time he's stolen a girlfriend. Mostly when we were teenagers, though."

"Funny best friend."

"Yeah. Well, I now have a vacancy for a new one." He smiled at her. "Although maybe now I have you I won't need anyone else."

"That's nice." Olivia smiled back. "But do you mind if I keep Jess? We're very close."

Adam laughed. "Of course. Jess is cool. Have you texted her yet?"

"What?"

"Texted her to tell her you're on your way to the Ritz?"

"Not yet. How d'you know I was going to?" Olivia wriggled a little.

"She's your best friend. You've probably been crying on her shoulder. Of course you're going to tell her. Do it now."

"Now?"

"Yes. Then I can have you all to myself all evening."

"Okay." Olivia grinned and pulled her phone out of her bag. She quickly wrote a message. *"On my way to the Ritz with Adam. Everything ok."* She added two smiley faces and pressed Send. "There, now I'm all yours. In fact, I'll turn the phone off."

"Wait until she's replied." Adam shook his head. "You know she will."

True to his word, the phone bleeped, and Olivia looked at the screen. She laughed. *"Yay! Livvy, Livvy, Livvy, that's awesome!!"* she read out. "Well, she's happy, then."

"And so am I." Adam was watching her as she turned the phone off and slipped it back into her bag. "And you have no idea just how much I want to kiss you right now."

"It can't be nearly as much as I want to kiss you." Olivia looked up at him, her heart beginning to beat faster again. "I've been dreaming of kissing you." And doing a lot more to you, too, she added silently, gazing into his eyes.

"But it's not really very private here." He jerked his head towards the uniformed chauffeur. "And we're nearly at the Ritz, so can you hang on just a little longer?"

"I guess I'll have to." She smiled up at him. "But not too long. You said we have a table booked. Are we not going to that party you mentioned?"

"That's not until later." Adam shrugged. "Well, it's on now, but I don't need to put in an appearance until later. We won't need to stay long, but I do need to show my face, since I'm the boss. Do you mind? We're having dinner on our own first."

"That's fine. But will I have to talk to lots of people?"

"We won't stay long, so probably not. Is it a problem?"

"I get a bit tongue-tied in those sorts of situations."

Olivia felt herself blushing again. "Sorry, that's a bit pathetic, isn't it?"

"Of course not. You're not used to things like that. Don't worry. You can stay with me. I'll look after you."

"Thank you. I'm a bit worried about it all being so posh. I shall probably use the wrong fork at dinner or something."

"Don't be daft. You can eat with your fingers if you like. I don't care. Look, we're here."

The limo had drawn up outside the entrance to the hotel, and a uniformed doorman came over and opened the door. Olivia stepped out onto the pavement.

"Good evening, miss." The doorman smiled at her. "Good evening, Mr. Munro. Do you have luggage?"

"Yes, there are a couple of bags in the boot. Thanks. My usual room." Adam took Olivia's hand and led her into the building.

"We're staying here?" she whispered to him in surprise.

"Yeah. Thought you might like it." He smiled down at her. "I told you the sort of dates I wanted to take you on. We're starting as I mean to go on. We're booked in for two nights, by the way. You don't need to be anywhere tomorrow, do you?"

She shook her head mutely and stared around her. It was every bit as magnificent as she had imagined, and she gripped tightly to Adam's hand as they walked towards the restaurant.

"It's nearly eight thirty." He glanced down at her. "Our table should be ready."

They were met at the door by a waiter who showed them to a table by the window, pulling Olivia's chair out for her. She sat down and looked around her while attempting not to make it too obvious.

The magnificent room with its sparkling chandeliers, marble columns, and a whole wall of mirrors seemed a world away from anything she had ever experienced before. Even the ceiling was beautifully painted with pink clouds drifting across a blue sky. The intimate tables were covered in pristine white cloths, and the chair she had been ushered into was upholstered in beautiful soft, pink velvet.

"Would you like some drinks, Mr. Munro?"

"Yes, please, a bottle of the Moet and Chandon Vintage Brut, thank you."

Olivia stared at him. "Champagne?" she whispered as the waiter moved away.

"Of course. You enjoyed that stuff at Christmas, didn't you? This is a better version." He reached across the table and took her hand. "Well. Here we are. I said I'd bring you here."

"And I must admit that for the last couple of days I was beginning to think it wouldn't happen. It still feels like a dream." She glanced around at the other diners. "This dress is okay, isn't it?"

"Of course it is. You look perfect. And extremely sexy." His eyes glinted. "Wait till you see our bedroom. Hope you didn't bring any pyjamas."

"Adam!" She giggled. "I have absolutely no idea what my mother packed. Knowing her, it could be quite embarrassing."

"Your mother seems really cool." He grinned. "I'd love to hear what you said about me. She was really giving me the onceover."

"She is a constant source of embarrassment to me." Olivia sighed with a smile. "But I love her to bits. We get on really well, and I can tell her nearly anything."

"Like what?" Adam sounded amused.

"Well, she asks awkward questions, and I just seem to end up answering them."

"So what did she ask about me?"

"You're very full of yourself, aren't you?" Olivia raised her eyebrows. "Not sure I should tell you."

"From the way she was looking at me, I rather suspect you told her what we did at the cottage."

Olivia looked down at her plate. "Maybe."

"Really? You tell your mother about sex?" Adam chuckled.

"She asked." Olivia sighed. "She asked if we had sex."

"And you said what?"

"Well, I tried to say no, but somehow ended up telling her what we actually *did* do. I'm sorry. Do you mind?" She looked up at him nervously.

"I don't mind, but did *she* mind?"

"Oh, god, no. She was enthralled. My mother lives her life entirely through romance novels and films. You heard what she said about *Love Actually*." She looked away for a moment. "Anyway, she was imagining all sorts. I had to tell her."

"What do you mean?" Adam was watching her, amusement clear in his face.

"Nothing." Olivia stared around the room. "This place is totally amazing. Thank you so much for bringing me here."

"Don't change the subject." Adam chuckled again. "What was she imagining?" He paused as the wine waiter appeared at his elbow and presented the bottle of Champagne. He nodded, and the man poured the sparkling wine into both their glasses, then moved away, leaving the bottle in an ice bucket next to their table. "Olivia? What was your mum thinking we were doing?"

Olivia glanced at him out of the corner of her eye. "She—well, she mentioned…"

"Mentioned what?" Adam was clearly enjoying her discomfort.

"Oh, hell. She mentioned *Fifty Shades of Grey.*"

Adam burst out laughing, and Olivia glanced around nervously in case anyone else had heard her. He reached across the table and took her hand. "Your mother sounds almost as unique as you," he said. "That is really funny." He lifted his Champagne glass and held it out towards her. "Now, Miss Marshall, what shall we drink to?"

"To us?" Olivia gave a shy smile and raised her glass. "To being back together."

"All right. To us, and to all the adventures we're going to have." They clinked their glasses together, and Olivia raised hers to her lips and took a sip. She looked up to find Adam watching her.

"You are so beautiful," he said softly, his eyes shining in the light of the candles. "I am so lucky to have found you."

"Thank you." She felt her face get hot and took another sip of Champagne. "But I think I'm the lucky one."

"Have you any idea what I'm thinking, right now?" He watched her across the table, gently twirling his glass in his hand.

Olivia shook her head, mesmerised by his piercing eyes. Her heart began to beat faster, and she felt her stomach do a flip as her mind flicked back to their time together in the cottage. She really hoped that was what he was thinking about.

"I was thinking just how nice it will be when we've finished dinner and can go up to our room. Just the two of us." He reached out and took her hand again, gently running his fingers over the palm. "Because I can think of some things we could practise until we got them completely perfect."

"We got pretty good at that neck thing." Olivia curled her fingers around his. "But I wouldn't mind practising it a bit more."

"Oh, I think we can do better than that." Adam's hand tightened over hers. "That was just the appetiser. You wait until the main course."

"Your menu, Madam."

Olivia jumped as the waiter held out the beautifully bound menu to her, and she pulled her hand away from Adam's. "Thank you." She opened it and stared down at the page. How could she possibly eat now he had implanted such thoughts in her head? All she wanted to do was go straight up to their room, rip all the clothes off his gorgeous body, and make love until the sun rose. And then again all day tomorrow.

She glanced over at Adam. He was looking down at his menu, but as she watched him he raised his head and smiled at her. Her stomach did another flip, and she began to get tingles all down her back as she remembered what he could do to her.

"What would you like to eat?"

"I don't know." She looked down at the menu again. "What do you recommend?"

"It's all good, but the lobster is especially nice. If

you like seafood."

"I do. Okay, then, I'll have the lobster."

"Don't you want a starter?"

She shook her head. "I think I shall have trouble eating anything, actually. I'm so sorry."

Adam shook his head. "Don't worry, I'm feeling the same way. The sooner this meal is out of the way the better." His gaze bored into her across the flickering candle flame. "And we can take the rest of the Champagne upstairs with us."

The waiter appeared at their side to take their order, and then Olivia leant forward towards Adam. "What about the party? Don't we have to go to that?"

"Damn." Adam frowned and ran a hand through his hair. "I forgot that. I'm afraid we do. But not for long. Can you bear it?"

"Of course." She smiled at him. "So long as we make it to the bedroom in the end."

"If I'd thought this through better"—Adam gave a crooked smile—"we would have gone to the party first, foregone dinner, and be in bed by now."

"Never mind. Anticipation is all part of the excitement." Olivia took a sip of her Champagne and licked her lips slowly. "Don't you agree?"

Adam groaned and shook his head. "Stop it. Why do you have to look so amazing? You don't want pudding, do you?"

"I don't even want the main course." Olivia smiled and took another sip of wine. "But it would be a bit rude if we didn't eat anything." She watched him through the candle flame. "I'm far more interested in the other main course you mentioned earlier."

Adam glanced around impatiently. "I wish they'd

hurry up with the lobster." He picked the Champagne bottle out of the ice bucket and topped up Olivia's glass. "I think we may need another bottle of this."

"It's really nice." She held the glass up to her face and let the bubbles tickle her nose. "I could get used to this."

"Good. I thought we should do this quite often." He watched her as she sipped the wine. "Make it a regular weekend treat?"

Olivia chuckled. "That sounds very decadent. I usually spend the weekend doing my washing."

"Well, I promised you afternoon tea here, didn't I? We could maybe have that tomorrow, actually." Adam glanced up as the waiter appeared again, and they both sat back as the lobster was served.

Chapter 14

"That was wonderful." Olivia sat back and wiped her mouth with her napkin. "Nice to know I like lobster."

"Yeah, I thought you would. Are you ready, then, or would you like something else?"

"No, thanks. No more food, anyway."

Adam got to his feet and smiled at her. "Good. That's exactly how I feel. Now let's get this bloody party out the way." He caught her hand with his left hand, fished the Champagne bottle out of the ice bucket with his right hand, and headed towards the door.

"Is it okay just to take that with us?" Olivia giggled as she tried to keep up with him.

"Why not? We paid for it. Not going to waste it." He ushered her towards a private room. "The party is in here, the Marie Antoinette Suite."

There was a uniformed porter at the door, and he nodded as they approached.

"Good evening, sir, madam. Should I announce you?"

Adam shook his head. "No, thanks. We're just putting in a quick appearance. I don't want any fuss." Still clutching Olivia's hand firmly in his, he walked into the room and glanced around. "Okay, hang on, this shouldn't take long. Just need them to see I was here."

As he moved down the room, a tall, heavily built

man approached them with his hand outstretched.

"Adam! Great to see you. We were wondering where you'd got to. Naomi has been here for ages."

"Naomi?" Adam stiffened and gripped Olivia's hand more tightly. "What the hell is she doing here?"

The man looked rather taken aback and frowned. "She's not here with you? She gave the impression she was."

"No." Adam's tone was curt. "As you can see, I'm here with Olivia. Olivia, this is Steven Morris, manager of the London office. Steve, this is my girlfriend, Olivia Marshall. Naomi and I broke up. There is no way she should be here tonight. Where is she?"

Steven gave Olivia's hand a limp shake and stared around. "I'm not sure. She was over with the Bristol lot just now…there, over there in the corner."

Adam looked down at Olivia. "I need to sort this. I'm so sorry, I have no idea what she's playing at. You stay here. I won't be long."

"I want to come with you." Olivia kept hold of his hand. "Let her see us together."

Adam paused and glanced at her. "Are you sure? She may not be very nice to you."

"I don't care. If you really want to be with me and she means nothing to you, then she should see us together."

"Of course I want to be with you." Adam squeezed her hand. "Don't ever doubt that. I just don't want you to get upset."

"I'm already upset. Your ex-girlfriend has turned up on our first date. It certainly wasn't what I had in mind, so I think I'd like to help sort it out."

Adam gave a brief nod and moved across the

crowded room to where Naomi was holding court to a group of partygoers. As they approached her, she looked up, and her face hardened as she saw Olivia clinging to Adam's hand.

"Naomi." Adam stopped in front of her. "May I have a word in private, please?"

"You can speak to me here, Adam." Naomi tossed her hair back and took a sip of her Champagne. "I have no secrets from these people. Do you?"

"As you wish." Adam raised an eyebrow. "What the hell are you doing here? Did you not realise when I broke up with you and asked you to leave my house that that also meant you would no longer be attending this party with me? Did I need to spell it out?"

There was a gasp from the group surrounding Naomi, and her face flushed an unbecoming shade of red.

"But I knew you didn't really mean it." She stared Adam straight in the eye. "I knew it was just a misunderstanding. I thought if I turned up here, we could sort things out." She narrowed her eyes at Olivia. "I didn't realise you'd be bringing someone else."

"A misunderstanding?" Adam's voice was deceptively calm. "You really want to do this here, Naomi? I fail to see how your actions could have been misunderstood." He glanced around at the mystified faces of his employees and then back at Naomi. "Are you going to leave now, or do you want me to go on? Tell these nice people what you actually did? Or will you just go now, believe me when I say it's all over, and not bother us again?"

Naomi looked away from him and placed her glass on a nearby table. "I shall leave," she said. "But this isn't over."

"Oh, yes, it is." Adam let go of Olivia's hand and stepped forward. "I need an assurance from you that you will let this go. Leave us to get on with our lives. It's over, and that's final."

"Who is this anyway?" Naomi's pale eyes ran dispassionately over Olivia. "Not your usual style."

"This is my girlfriend, Olivia." Adam caught her hand again. "And if you say anything derogatory about her, I shall have no compunction in announcing to the whole room what you did. Now please leave. I can call you a cab, if you like."

Naomi stared at them both with unconcealed dislike. "I'll go. I can call my own cab."

"And you'll leave us alone?"

She didn't answer and started walking towards the door.

"Naomi? I need you to answer me."

"Fuck off." She didn't look round. "I'm not one of your sodding employees. You can't tell me what to do. I'm going. That's what you wanted." She reached the door and swung through it without a backward glance, pushing past the doorman.

"Are you all right?" Adam looked down at Olivia and slipped his arm around her shoulders. "I'm sorry about that."

"It's not your fault." Olivia's eyes were fixed on the door. "She hasn't given up, you know."

"I know." He turned to the group of guests beside them. "I'm sorry about that, guys. Naomi and I broke up just before Christmas, but for some reason she doesn't seem to have got the message. Now, please have some more Champagne and enjoy the party."

Catching Olivia by the hand again, Adam made his way towards a small raised stage area in the corner, where a four-piece band were playing some light jazz. He let go of her hand, hopped onto the stage, and murmured something into the ear of the bandleader. After a moment, the band stopped playing and Adam stepped forward. He smiled around at the assembled guests.

"Hi, everyone. So glad you could all be here tonight, and I hope you're enjoying it so far. The entertainment will be carrying on until after midnight, and I believe a light finger buffet supper will be served at around eleven. I'm afraid I won't be able to stay for the whole thing, but thanks for coming, and have a great time." He paused and grinned around the room. "And I hope to see some of you full of the joys of the New Year on Monday, back in Bristol."

There was a rumble of laughter from one side of the room, and a cheer went up. Adam laughed. "And I'm sure we'll have another party when we're all back there, too. See you later, guys, and have fun." He waved a hand, and stepping back down off the platform, he caught Olivia by the hand again and headed for the door, pausing a couple of times to shake hands with his employees before leaving the room and making their way back towards the lifts.

Olivia glanced up at him as they stood waiting for the lift. As well as the upsetting scene with Naomi, she had seen another side of him, and she was feeling rather overwhelmed. Suddenly he wasn't the stranger she had rescued from the beach and kept. He was the big boss of a huge multi-million-pound business, and from the reaction of the people in the room, he was well loved by his employees. He was only a couple of years older than her, yet he commanded respect from hundreds of people. And he seemed to take it all in his stride. No wonder he had found the playacting over Christmas so easy.

"What's wrong? Is it Naomi? I'm really sorry about that, but I don't think she'll bother us again."

She found he was watching her, a slight frown creasing his brow.

"No. Not Naomi. No, nothing's wrong."

"Yes, there is. Olivia? Tell me, what's wrong?"

She looked away from him. "You just seemed so…so…different in there. So in charge." She turned to face him. "It just suddenly struck me who you are. The boss of a huge multinational company, and I'm a primary school teacher from Essex. What can we possibly have in common?"

He stared at her and moved a couple of paces closer. "You can honestly ask that, after spending those days together? Surely it was obvious what we have in common."

She shook her head. "You mean the fact that we fancy the shit out of each other?"

Adam gave a short laugh. "Well, that too, I guess, but no, I didn't mean that." He took her hands in his and pulled her even closer. "I mean the fact that we understand each other. We have the same sense of humour and we were able to slot into the roles we played over Christmas with no problem. We're meant to be together, and although I hate to say it, not just for the sex. Although I have a feeling that's going to be a very enjoyable part of our relationship."

He pulled her right up against him, pinning her arms to her sides. "You see, I really like you. As a person. I want to spend time with you, and I thought you wanted to spend time with me. Please don't be intimidated by the job. That's only a tiny part of who I am."

Olivia looked up at him, her body now pressed against his. She could feel her heart start to beat faster, and she nodded. "I know it is. But it's rather a scary part. Of course I want to spend time with you, and when I thought you weren't coming back, I was..." She hesitated over the word. "I was, quite honestly. devastated. So yes, I really like you too. So if you don't think it matters that we're from different worlds, then I guess I can try not to be scared by it."

"Good." He smiled down at her. "That's got that sorted. Now, here's the lift coming. I can't wait for you to see our room. I think you're really going to love it."

Olivia chuckled. "You look like a kid when you get excited. I'm dying to see our room. Does it have a nice big bed?"

"Of course." He let go of her as the lift doors opened and stood aside for her to get in. "It's a king size."

She was just about to step into the lift when the sound of an enormous explosion shook the whole foyer of the hotel, and Adam caught her arm to steady her.

"What the hell...?" He spun round to face the door, and they could see huge plumes of smoke billowing out from across the street. Together they joined the group of other guests who had run towards the sound but stopped short in the doorway.

A huge explosion had ripped the front off the building directly opposite the hotel, and broken glass and burning debris was falling down into the road below. The traffic had come to a standstill, and the sound of horns blaring and terrified screaming rent the night air. Several cars were on fire, and terrified travellers and pedestrians were fleeing in all directions.

"Oh, god!" Olivia put her hand over her mouth and stared at the scene in horror. "Oh, god, was that a bomb? We must do something."

Adam held her arm tightly. "Stay here," he ordered. "It's not safe out there. We have no idea what caused it. I'll go and see if I can help, but you stay here."

Olivia shook his hand off her arm. "If you're going out there, so am I. I have a first aid certificate, remember? We have to help. Look, other people are going."

"Stay here," he repeated, glancing at her. "Please, do as I say. I'm just going to see what's going on." He placed a quick kiss on her lips and then ran out into the chaotic street, accompanied by a group of guests and hotel employees.

Olivia hesitated for just a moment, then followed them outside, her eyes immediately taking in the carnage all around her. The whole front of the building across the road had blown out, and flames were billowing from the upper floors. Falling debris had set fire to several cars that were now lying abandoned, their owners sheltering in the doorways of nearby buildings. All the traffic had come to a standstill, and the distant sound of sirens could be heard above the screams of those caught up in the disaster.

She stared around her for Adam and saw him over by a car that had slid across the road and come to a halt against a bollard. He appeared to be helping the passengers climb out of the vehicle.

Glancing around to see if there was anyone she could help, her eyes fell almost immediately on a girl sitting on the edge of the pavement, her head bowed and her long blonde hair falling over her face. She was clutching her arm, and Olivia could make out blood seeping through her fingers. She picked her way carefully across to her and squatted down.

"Are you hurt? Can I help you?"

The girl didn't look up, and her voice was shaking. "My arm. Something hit it. I can't stop the bleeding."

Gently Olivia took the girl's arm in her hands, seeing immediately a deep cut just above the elbow. It was bleeding heavily, and she searched around for something to press over it. "Do you have a jacket or anything?" she asked, carefully wiping the worst of the blood away with some tissues from her bag.

The girl shook her head. "No. Nothing. Is it really bad?" Her voice was shaking, and Olivia put a hand on her shoulder to calm her.

"Not too bad. We need to stop the bleeding, but it's easily sortable. You'll need a couple of stitches. When the ambulances arrive, I'll see you get taken to the hospital."

In the absence of anything else, Olivia untied the sash from around her dress and folded it up so one end formed a thick pad. She placed it gently against the cut and wound the rest of the material around the girl's arm. She pressed on it firmly and knelt down on the pavement beside her. "Do you think you could put your hand on here?" she asked. "Then I can go and see if I can help anyone else. You'll be okay."

"Please don't go." The girl reached out with her

other hand and grabbed Olivia's wrist. "I'm really scared."

"Okay. Okay. Don't worry, you'll be fine. Is there anyone with you? Can I find someone for you?" For the first time, she looked closely at the girl's face and gasped with shock. "Naomi?"

The girl looked up and peered at her through the smoke. She closed her eyes and sighed. "Oh. It's you."

"What were you doing out here? I thought you'd gone to get a cab." Olivia took a look at the wound and adjusted the makeshift bandage slightly.

"I decided to walk." Naomi spoke very quietly. "I needed to think. To clear my head." She looked up at Olivia again. "Where's Adam? Is he really angry with me?"

Olivia hesitated for a moment, then nodded. "Yeah. Yeah, he is. Surely you're not surprised. What on earth were you doing here tonight?"

"I thought if I turned up…" Naomi shivered. "I just thought I might be able to explain to him. Make him come back."

"You're cold. I think you may be in shock. Let me take you into the hotel." Olivia took her arm.

"No. I don't want to go back in there." Naomi shook her head. "I'm okay. I've been really stupid. I know that. I just thought maybe I could persuade Adam…" She tailed off and looked up at Olivia again. "Then I saw him with you. That really got to me. I could see how much he likes you." She looked away and stared over at the burning building. "He never looked at me like that. Where is he? I want to apologize."

"He's helping some people over there." Olivia

waved her arm towards the car she had seen earlier. "You don't need to do that. I can tell him."

"He's not in danger, is he?" There was a note of panic in Naomi's voice, and Olivia glanced down at her.

"I hope not. I'm trying not to think about that." She got to her feet and stared across the street. Almost at once Adam appeared from behind a car and stared back at her. He moved across the debris-strewn road towards her.

"I told you to stay in the hotel." He reached her and caught her by the shoulders. "It's not safe out here. For all we know, there may be more explosions. Go back in."

"No. Adam, look." She pointed to Naomi, hunched up on the pavement, her head lowered. "Naomi is injured. I've been looking after her."

Adam moved over towards the girl and squatted down in front of her. "Naomi? What the hell are you still doing here? Olivia says you're injured."

She raised her head and stared at him. "My arm. Olivia has fixed it. Adam..." Her voice cracked, and she looked away. "Adam, I'm sorry. I behaved really badly. I'm so sorry I came here tonight. I won't bother you again. I can see how you feel about Olivia."

Adam reached out and took her hand. "Thank you. Now, however angry I was with you, I don't want to see you hurt. Is she going to be okay, Olivia?"

"Yes." Olivia squatted down beside them, wishing he would let go of Naomi's hand. "She'll need some stitches, but she'll be okay. I've stemmed the bleeding. I'll wait with her until the ambulances arrive."

Adam nodded and let go of her hand. He stood up

and caught Olivia by the arm, pulling her up with him. "I really wish you'd go back in, but I can see you're not going to, so please, please, be vigilant and stay back from the fire. Stay with her until the paramedics arrive, and then you're to go in."

Olivia stared at him. His face was streaked with black and his bowtie had come undone. If anything, he looked even more handsome, and despite the situation she felt her body start to tingle. She was beginning to think they would never make it to the bedroom.

"Are you being careful?" she managed. "I saw you help some people out of a car."

"Yeah. A few people got trapped when debris fell on their vehicles." He glanced back over his shoulder. "I need to go and see if there are any more. I'll be careful." He leaned forward and placed a quick kiss on her lips and then turned and headed towards an estate car that was partly crushed against the wall of the opposite building.

Olivia watched him go, her heart leaping into her throat. He was going very close to the source of the explosion, and she desperately wanted to reach out to him and pull him back to the safety of the hotel. Instead, she sank down onto the pavement next to Naomi and checked the girl's wound again. It had started to bleed a little more, so she adjusted the bandage again and applied more pressure. Naomi had gone very white, and Olivia peered at her in concern.

"Do you feel faint?"

"No. I'm all right. Just feel cold." She glanced at Olivia. "You probably hate me, but please will you stay with me?"

"Of course I will." Olivia's eyes were following

Adam's movements on the other side of the road. "And it's probably you who should hate me."

"I do." Naomi managed a small smile. "But it's my own fault, so I shall have to live with it. I think you'll probably make him a lot happier than I would have done. Than I did. Promise me you will?"

"I hope I will." Olivia looked at her in surprise. "He makes me very happy."

"That car is very close to the fire." Naomi was watching the car Adam was standing by. "What's he doing?"

"He's helping some trapped people out." Olivia stood up again and stared across the road. As she watched, Adam reached in through the back window of the car and appeared to be struggling with something. Someone shouted to him, and he pulled his head out and glanced down at the road under the car. Another man ran over to join him, and they both struggled to pull the door open. It resisted, and Adam put his head through the window again.

"What's happening?" Naomi had struggled to her feet and swayed dangerously. Olivia caught her arm, and together they stood and stared at the scene across the road.

"I think he's trying to get someone out." Olivia peered more closely through the dark and the smoke. "But I think there's a problem. He was looking at the ground under the car just now. Stay there." She moved a few steps nearer, and her heart leapt into her mouth as she saw the rapidly spreading puddle of petrol that was leaking out from the bottom of the car. "Shit."

She glanced behind her. Naomi had sunk back down onto the pavement, and a paramedic from one of the recently arrived ambulances had bent down beside her. Trusting that she would now be all right, Olivia took another step forward, her hands pressed over her mouth.

Adam was still struggling to manoeuvre someone out of the car through the window, and the petrol had nearly reached the burning building. She held her breath as she saw another person's head appear in the window of the car and Adam attempted to pull them out.

"Get back, love! That car's about to blow."

Olivia found herself being pulled back onto the pavement by a paramedic, and struggled against his grip. "No, let me go. My boyfriend is over there! Let me go!"

The man tightened his grip and shook his head. "Can't let you do that. It's leaking petrol, and it's nearly reached the fire. It's going to go up at any second." As he finished speaking, there was an almighty explosion and the car became a ball of fire, debris flying everywhere.

"Adam!" Olivia heard herself screaming as she struggled against the strong grip of the paramedic. "Let me go! Adam! Oh, god, no!"

"Stay here. Don't struggle." The man held her tighter. "There's nothing you can do."

As she watched, several newly arrived firemen raced over to the vehicle and attempted to put the fire out. Tears now streaming down her cold cheeks, she gave up struggling against the man's grip and stared transfixed through the smoke and flames at what remained of the car. It was surrounded by firemen and a cordon of police who were attempting to keep the public back, and as she watched through her tears, a cheer went up and a figure emerged from the smoke and flames carrying someone in their arms.

Olivia held her breath and pulled free from the arms of the paramedic. "Adam?" she whispered, hardly daring to hope. "Adam!" She moved towards the figures just as a paramedic darted out and took the child from the arms of his rescuer. "Adam?"

They walked towards each other, and Olivia held her breath as she stared at him. His face was almost black with smoke, his shirt ripped down the front, and his hair slightly singed and full of black debris. She swallowed a huge lump in her throat and stopped in front of him. He stared at her for a moment, then pulled her towards him and held her tightly, pressing his face into her hair.

"I thought you were dead," she whispered, her arms clinging around him and her face buried in his shoulder. "I saw the car explode...I thought..." She felt his lips come down on hers, and she tasted the strong acrid smoke on his skin as he pressed closer, his arms tightening around her.

"Sir? May we check you over? You had a very narrow escape."

They pulled apart, and Olivia looked up to see a paramedic there watching Adam with concern. He shook his head.

"I'm fine. You go and deal with the injured. There are plenty of them. How's the child?"

"He'll be fine." The paramedic smiled. "Thanks to you. He's over in the ambulance. I think his mother would like to speak to you. And we really must check you over."

Adam shook his head, sending up a cloud of ash and black particles. "No. I'm fine. I need to go and check the other cars."

"No, not now, sir. The emergency services are all here now, and the public are being moved to safety. Your help has been much appreciated, but the fire brigade and police are taking over. Now, please come over to the ambulance for a moment." The paramedic took his arm and encouraged him to go with her. Adam resisted, and Olivia put her hand on his arm.

"Adam, this isn't like the beach. I can't check you over this time. You were just nearly blown up. Please let them check you over. You may have some burns."

He looked down at her and shrugged. "Okay, if I must. I want to check on the child anyway." He reached out, took Olivia's hand, and held it very tightly. She squeezed it back and walked very close to him, horrified to find there were still tears rolling down her cheeks. Glancing up at him, she saw that under the layer of grime, his face was very white, and his hand was shaking slightly in hers. She held his arm with her other hand and looked up at him.

"Are you all right?"

He nodded. "Yeah. Just feel a bit wobbly."

They had reached one of the ambulances, and the paramedic made Adam sit down while she checked him over.

"Where's the boy I got out of the car? I'd like to see him."

"He's in the ambulance. We're taking him to the hospital. He has a broken ankle and some bruising. You can see him in a minute." She started wiping some of the grime from his face and arms in order to check for any injuries. Olivia stood beside him, aware of how tightly he was still gripping her hand. She smiled down at him, and he stared back. "Does anything hurt?" The paramedic was peering into his eyes. "How do you feel?"

"I'm fine. Just feel a bit shaky, and my face is stinging a bit. And I'm cold."

"Hardly surprising you feel shaky. You nearly got blown up." She smiled. "I think it would be best if we took you in to the hospital for observation and to get you cleaned up. Your face has some surface burns. Nothing that will scar, but it may be sore for a few days."

"No. I'm not going to hospital. I'm fine. My girlfriend can look after me." He held even tighter to Olivia's hand. "She's done a first aid course."

"Adam, I think you should do as they say." Olivia looked down at him. "You know my course was very basic. I think they should keep an eye on you overnight."

"Have I got a head injury?"

"No." The paramedic shook her head. "Just a few surface burns."

"Then I'm not coming with you. If I haven't got a head injury, I'm not in any danger of dropping dead." He smiled up at Olivia. "So I'm going to stay here. With you. You can make sure I'm okay."

Olivia looked over at the paramedic. "Will that be okay? Will he be all right?"

The woman looked back at Adam for a moment, then shrugged. "Almost certainly yes," she said, "but you need to keep an eye on him for symptoms of shock. It's very unlikely, but just to be sure. Here, I have a leaflet…" She delved into a bag beside her and pulled out a sheet of paper. "It says here what to watch out for, and what to do if he gets any symptoms. Bring him straight to hospital if he does display any symptoms. Do you have far to go?"

"We're staying at the Ritz." Olivia felt her face flush. "It was supposed to be a special night."

The paramedic smiled. "Well, probably special for a different reason now. Your boyfriend is a hero. If he hadn't done what he did, the child in the ambulance back there would be dead, not just suffering from a broken ankle." She turned to Adam. "Would you like to see the boy now?"

Adam nodded and got to his feet. "Yes, please. Just to check he's really all right. He was so scared in the car." Letting go of Olivia's hand, he stepped up into the ambulance, glancing back over his shoulder. "Wait there for me. Please."

Olivia watched him disappear into the ambulance, a lump forming in her throat. He suddenly looked so vulnerable. So different from the confident boss he had been an hour ago. She swallowed and turned to the paramedic. "Do they know what caused the explosion? Was it a bomb?"

"No, not this time. Apparently they think it was a gas leak." The paramedic was watching through the door of the ambulance. "That's what I heard, anyway. But also from what I've heard, thanks to the quick action of people like your boyfriend no one has died tonight. We got here as quickly as we could, but without the help from the public, things could have been very different."

She paused as Adam appeared in the doorway of

the ambulance and stepped back down into the road. "All right?"

He nodded. "Yes. He's going to be fine. I just needed to be sure." He sighed. "His mother wouldn't leave me alone. Kept wanting to know my name."

"Of course she did." Olivia caught his hand. "You saved her child. She's never going to forget you. Did you tell her your name?"

"I just said Adam. She doesn't need to know any more." He looked down at her. "If I really can't do any more to help, can we go to the hotel now? I'm beginning to feel a lie-down would be nice."

Olivia nodded and smiled at the paramedic. "Thanks for your help." As they started to walk away towards the Ritz, she hesitated and let go of Adam's hand. "Hang on a sec. Stay there." She turned back and caught the paramedic as she was moving towards another patient. "Sorry to bother you, but have you seen a blonde girl in a red dress? She had an arm injury."

The paramedic paused for a moment, then nodded. "Yes, yes, I think I have. She had a rather strange blue bandage on her arm."

"That was the sash off my dress." Olivia smiled. "Is she okay?"

"She will be. She lost a fair amount of blood, and she'll need quite a few stitches, but she'll be fine. Is she a friend of yours?"

Olivia smiled. "No. Not a friend. I just helped her. Wanted to be sure she was all right. Thanks." She hurried back and joined Adam, catching his hand in hers.

"What were you doing?" He looked down at her, his eyes screwed up against the smoke.

"Just checking Naomi was all right. Now, come on, let's get you cleaned up." She led the way back into the hotel and headed towards the lifts. The foyer was swarming with people, many taking shelter from the carnage out in the road, and as Olivia and Adam wended their way through them, they were approached by the hotel manager.

"Mr. Munro, are you all right, sir?"

"Fine, thank you." Adam swayed slightly and gripped Olivia's hand more tightly. "We're going up to our room."

"Of course, sir. If there's anything you need, just call room service."

"Thank you." Olivia smiled at him, and they moved over towards the lifts.

The lift doors opened as they approached, and they stepped inside, Adam immediately pressing the button for the fifth floor. As the doors closed, he leaned back against the wall and shut his eyes. Olivia moved to his side and took his hand.

"Are you all right?"

"I will be." He didn't open his eyes. "Just need to get cleaned up and have a lie-down. My eyes and face are really stinging now."

"I'm not surprised." Olivia was watching him with concern. "I wish you'd agreed to go to the hospital, though."

He opened his eyes and looked down at her. "What is it with you and hospitals? I didn't need one at Christmas, and I don't need one now. I just need to lie down, and if you think I'm missing our night together, you have another think coming."

The lift slowed as it reached their floor, and he

pushed himself upright. "Wait till you see our room. You're going to love it." He stood aside for her to leave the lift, then took her hand again and led her towards a door at the end of the corridor. "Welcome to your home for the next two days."

As she stepped into the huge room, Olivia caught her breath. It was furnished all in blue, and the enormous bed dominated the room. It was more like a living room than a bedroom, with several sofas and coffee tables, and a large flat-screen TV.

"It's wonderful." She stared around her and moved towards the bed. "Absolutely brilliant. Bit different to that bedroom in the cottage!"

"Just a bit." Adam had come up behind her, and she could feel his breath on her neck. "Pretty sure the bed will work the same way, though." He walked over to it and sat down heavily on the edge. "Sorry, I don't think my legs are going to hold me up much longer. Don't know why, but they're feeling rather like jelly."

"You don't know why?" Olivia moved over and sat down next to him. "You were very nearly blown up. You escaped death by seconds less than half an hour ago. If you didn't feel a bit wobbly, I'd be worried."

"I suppose you're right." He sighed and bowed his head. "It was actually very scary. And all I could think about was you. How I was letting you down."

"What?" Olivia put her hand on his arm. "Why on earth did you think that? You were rescuing someone. I'm sure it was terrifying, but why on earth did you think you were letting me down?"

He looked up at her, and she felt tears well up again as she saw his face in the full light. Under the layer of dirt, it was red and raw in places, and his eyes were bloodshot. He swallowed. "I honestly couldn't see how I was going to get out of that alive, and you were watching, and…and I couldn't bear it. But I couldn't leave the child. He was injured and terrified, and he was relying on me to save him." He looked away. "I couldn't let him die alone."

Olivia put her arm around his shoulders and held his hand tightly. "I know you couldn't. Of course you couldn't. But you did save him. He's going to be all right because of you."

"But I nearly left you." His voice cracked. "I nearly left you, and I didn't want to. I really, really didn't want to. But I couldn't abandon him. He was so trusting that I'd save him." He turned and buried his face in her shoulder, his arms holding her close.

"I know." Olivia stroked his smoke-blackened hair gently. "I know. And it was truly awful, seeing the car explode. The worst moment of my life. I watched it happen, and I could do nothing. One of the paramedics was actually holding me back." She took a long shuddering breath. "I still don't understand how you escaped."

Adam pulled back from her and wiped a hand across his eyes. "I managed to pull him through the window just before it went up, and when the car actually exploded, we had just turned our backs on it. I felt the blast, of course, but I just held the child tight and ran." He took a deep breath. "I don't think it's going to be easy to get the images out of my mind."

"I imagine not." Olivia watched him with concern. "I really wish you'd gone to the hospital. But you didn't, so you must let me look after you."

"That's what I want."

"Okay. First you need to get out of those clothes and get showered. Or would you prefer a bath?"

"A shower will do." He got to his feet and began to peel off his jacket. "Not much left of this shirt."

Olivia smiled at him. "This is probably going to sound very inappropriate, but you still look amazing. The sexy hero."

"Don't say that." Adam tossed the ruined shirt into the corner. "I'm not a hero. I only did what anyone would have done." He glanced at her and managed a small smile. "You can say I'm sexy, though, if you like."

"Of course you're a hero." Olivia stood up and walked over to him. "And very few people would have done what you did. It was very brave." She stood on tiptoe and kissed him on the cheek. "Now, go and get cleaned up. Do you want anything to drink, or eat?"

"Nothing to eat." He shook his head. "Maybe a cup of coffee would be nice. You can order one from room service."

"You go and shower, and I'll have it ready for you." Olivia gave him a gentle shove towards the bathroom. "I'm just going to put the TV on, see if there's anything about the explosion. And I'd better text my parents, in case they've heard about it." She watched him get into the shower, then sat down on the bed and fished her phone out of her bag. She turned it back on and saw she had ten missed calls and seven texts. With a grimace, she read the first text. It was from her mother.

"We saw the explosion. Are you all right?"

The second message was from Jess, saying almost the same, and the following ones were all slightly more urgent versions of the first ones. Olivia wrote a reply and sent it to both of them.

"Sorry, phone was off. We're okay. It was dreadful. Adam was a hero. Talk tomorrow. Back in hotel now."

She placed the phone on the bedside table, kicked her shoes off, and turned on the TV. Flicking through the channels, she very quickly came to a news one showing pictures of the street outside the hotel. She turned up the sound and sat forward to watch.

"A massive explosion, thought to have been caused by a gas leak, ripped through a building opposite the Ritz Hotel in Piccadilly this evening. The street was busy with New Year's Eve revellers, and a number of cars were destroyed by the fire. So far the number of people injured is around fifty, but thanks to the quick action of some members of the public, no one is thought to have died."

The presenter turned to a woman at her side. "This lady's son would have died when the family car he was trapped in exploded, had it not been for the bravery of one particular bystander. Apparently the man stayed with the child and managed to extract him through the window of the car just as the vehicle caught fire and exploded." The camera moved to the woman beside her, and the presenter held the microphone out to her. "Do you have anything to say to the rescuer?"

The woman nodded, her eyes shiny with tears. "I can never thank him enough. He saved my boy…" Her voice faltered, and she blew her nose with a screwed-up tissue. "Without him, my son would have died a horrible death. We'll be forever in his debt. Thank you."

The presenter smiled at her. "And did you find out his name?"

"Just his first name. Adam." The woman looked directly at the camera. "Whoever and wherever you are, Adam, thank you. Thank you."

Olivia muted the sound and stared at the screen. She knew if she just went over to the window she could look down on the scene more or less as it appeared on the screen. She slid off the bed and walked over to the window, pulling the curtains across without looking down, and then went over to call room service.

Adam was still in the shower, so she lifted her overnight bag onto the bed and rummaged inside to see what her mother had packed. To her surprise, it was all fairly sensible stuff, and she pulled out an oversized T-shirt to wear in bed. Once Adam had finished in the bathroom, she would pop in, have a quick wash, and clean her teeth. She would have a bath in the morning.

The coffee had just arrived when Adam emerged from the shower, rubbing his hair with a towel. Now his face was clean, she was shocked to see just how red and sore it looked. The front of his hair was noticeably singed, and his eyes looked puffy and bloodshot.

"Here's your coffee." She put it on the bedside table and looked up at him. "Does that feel any better? Your face and eyes look very sore."

"They are." He dropped the towel on the floor and sat down on the bed. "Just saw myself in the mirror. I hope it doesn't put you off."

"Don't be daft." Olivia smiled at him. "Nothing could do that. I do feel very sorry for you, though. It'll probably be sore for quite a few days. I think you should probably go to the doctor's tomorrow."

"New Year's Day?"

"Oh. Right. I'd forgotten. Oh, well, maybe pop to A&E, then. They could give you something to put on your face."

"Maybe." Adam shrugged and slid up the bed until he was leaning against the pillows. He picked up his coffee and took a sip. "That's nice. God, I'm tired. Was there anything on the news about it?"

"Yes." Olivia nodded, wondering how much to tell him. "They said about fifty people were injured, but no one died."

"That's good."

"They said it was because of members of the public helping."

Adam took another sip of coffee. "Okay."

"They interviewed the mother of the boy you saved."

"Glad I didn't see that."

"She kept saying thank you to you."

He put his cup down and slid under the covers. "I don't really want to think about it now. Are you coming to bed? Take my mind off it all."

"Yes, of course." Olivia smiled at him. "I'll just go and clean my teeth. Won't be a sec." She went into the bathroom, closed the door, and leaned against it. She still felt very shaken by the events of the last hour and couldn't even begin to imagine how Adam must be feeling.

Part of her was very worried that he hadn't gone to the hospital, but another part was selfishly pleased he hadn't. She quite enjoyed looking after him, although she was a little worried by just how vulnerable he was looking.

She cleaned her teeth, washed her face and hands, and took a deep breath. It was her job to see he got a good night's sleep. Clearly the evening wasn't going quite the way either of them had imagined, but at least they would be sleeping in the same bed.

Opening the door, she stepped back into the bedroom and bit her lip as she stared at the bed. Adam was fast asleep, curled up on his side, the quilt pulled up over his shoulder.

Quietly Olivia got in beside him and turned off the light. She slid down under the covers and reached out her hand, entwining her fingers loosely with his. She wriggled into the middle of the bed and gently put her arm across him.

He moved slightly in his sleep, and she tightened her grip.

She would keep him safe.

Chapter 15

New Year's Day

Olivia opened her eyes slowly and rolled onto her back. It took her a moment to realise where she was, and then she looked over to her left. The bed was empty beside her, the cover thrown back. She raised herself up onto her elbows and looked around the room. Adam was standing at the window, staring down at the street below. He was still wearing the T-shirt and boxers he had slept in.

"Morning."

He turned to face her. "Good morning. Did you sleep all right?" He walked over and sat down on the edge of the bed.

"Not too bad." Olivia hesitated. "Just a couple of disturbances."

"Was that me?"

"Yeah." She nodded. "I think you were having bad dreams."

He pulled back the cover and got in beside her, sliding down until their faces were just inches apart. "Yes. I did. Sorry if I woke you."

"Don't be daft. Are you all right this morning? Your face and eyes look much better."

"They feel it. My eyes are fine, and my face just stings a bit." He put out a hand and hooked her hair behind her ear. "I'm sorry we didn't get our night of passion last night."

"Again, don't be daft." Olivia moved a little closer to him. "Happy New Year."

"Oh, so it is. Happy New Year." Adam put his arms around her and pulled her even closer. "Shall we try and make it a really happy one?"

"Sounds good to me."

"What do you want to do today?" Adam's hands had started to move over her body, and Olivia felt herself stiffen in anticipation.

"What we're doing right now seems pretty good," she murmured, leaning forward and pressing her lips gently against his. "Do your lips hurt, or is this okay?"

"It's fine." His hot breath was entering her mouth and mingling with her own, and Olivia shuddered with desire, her whole body tingling from his touch.

She ran her hands down his torso, pressing ever closer, their lips still together and their tongues entwining.

"May I undress you?" Her words were muffled by the kissing. "It would make this even more interesting."

Adam pulled back slightly. "Of course. Then may I return the favour?" His fingers were gently flicking across her nipples through her thin T-shirt.

"You may." Olivia pushed back the cover and got up on her knees. She rolled Adam onto his back and gently eased his T-shirt over his head, then ran her hands down his body until she reached the top of his boxers. Very slowly she slid her finger around inside the waistband, at the same time straddling his legs and holding them down.

He sucked in his breath and closed his eyes. She

ran her finger around again, this time going a little lower down, and he gave a little moan of pleasure. Gently she eased his boxers off and lay full length on top of his naked body, fastening her lips onto his again.

With one swift movement, Adam rolled her over and hovered above her, his gaze boring into her. Without breaking eye contact, he pulled her T-shirt over her head and slid her panties off, gently running his hands all over her body. He lay down beside her and pulled her so close their bodies were pressed hard against each other.

Olivia slid her arms around him and ran her fingers down his spine at the same time as he began to caress the back of her neck. Immediately her whole body fizzed with desire, and she arched her back so their bodies pressed even closer and she could feel the full extent of his desire for her. Their mouths met again as he rolled her onto her back and lowered himself onto her, still caressing her neck as he gently entered her.

She gasped with desire and pulled him down on top of her, her fingers raking at his back and her breath coming in ragged gasps as the orgasm took hold and carried her into ecstasy. They climaxed simultaneously, their bodies slick with sweat, and stayed, still clasped together, hearts thumping uncontrollably.

Olivia lay with her eyes closed, Adam's head cradled on her shoulder and her arms wrapped tightly around him. It had been totally amazing, and without doubt the best sex she had ever had. She opened her eyes and looked down at him.

"That was amazing," she whispered, her lips pressed into his hair. "But I think we may need to practise it some more. What do you think?"

Adam lifted his head and stared at her. "Without a doubt," he said solemnly. "Probably quite a lot, actually. Give me five minutes, and we can start as we mean to go on."

Olivia gave a little chuckle, put her arms around his neck, and stared him in the eyes. "You are amazing, too. I still keep thinking I'm dreaming. What the hell am I, Olivia Marshall, doing lying in a huge bed in the Ritz with the most gorgeous man in the universe? How did that happen?"

"Well, I think it all started when you found me on the beach and kept me..." Adam grinned at her. "And I'm the one who can't believe it's true. You really are the most beautiful girl in the world, and you're mine." He looked suddenly uncertain. "Or I hope you are? I hope I'm not presuming too much?"

"How could you even think that?" Olivia pulled him closer, her lips almost touching his. "Don't you realise how I feel about you?"

"I can only hope," he murmured. "I know how I feel about you. Olivia Marshall, I love you."

Olivia felt her body start to tingle again, and a lump appeared in her throat. "I love you too," she managed. "I love you too."

Epilogue

23rd June

"Happy birthday."

Olivia opened her eyes sleepily and found Adam sitting on the edge of the bed, smiling at her. She pushed herself up on her elbow and yawned. "Thank you. Have I slept late?"

"Not really." He shrugged and leant down to kiss her. "I've ordered breakfast for nine, so I thought I'd better wake you."

"Breakfast in the room? That's a treat." She struggled into a sitting position and glanced towards the window. "It looks like another lovely day. Thank you so much for bringing me here. It was the perfect birthday present."

"Oh, this isn't your present." Adam got up and grinned down at her. "I promised you a trip to Venice for your birthday back at Christmas. You were always going to have that. Your present is still to come."

Olivia pushed the pillows up behind her and got comfortable. "Really? Now I'm excited all over again. When can I have it?"

"All in good time." Adam laughed and walked over to the window. He stared down at the Grand Canal, the water glistening in the early morning sun. "We're going on a gondola later. Can't come to Venice and not do that."

"Awesome. Is that my present, then?"

"No. Be patient." He turned and smiled at her again. "Our breakfast should be here any minute."

"So do I have to wait until after breakfast for my present?" Olivia wriggled impatiently.

Adam moved towards the door as a light tap sounded, and opened it to reveal a waiter with a trolley. He stood aside to let them in, and had the trolley wheeled up to beside the bed. He tipped the waiter, and then walked over to the bed.

"Champagne?" Olivia stared at the bottle in surprise. "For breakfast? That's a bit decadent."

"It's for Buck's Fizz." Adam uncorked the bottle and deftly mixed two tall glasses with freshly squeezed orange juice. He handed one to Olivia. "Here you go. Don't drink it yet, just put it by the bed."

She glanced suspiciously at him but placed the glass on the bedside table. "Okay. Why?"

"We'll have a toast in a minute." He looked at her solemnly. "To a couple of things, actually. Do you realise that not only is it your birthday but it's also the six-month anniversary of the day we met? So we have a few things to celebrate. Now, shall I give you your present now, or wait until you've eaten? That's a conundrum, isn't it? What do you think I should do?"

"Now!" Olivia bounced up and down like a child. "I can't wait any longer."

"But you may be disappointed. It may not be what you want."

"Of course it will." She stared at him in surprise. "I could never be disappointed with anything you gave me. Just being here with you was enough of a present.

Anything else is a bonus. But I would like it before I eat."

Adam chuckled. "Okay, then. Although I am a little nervous about this. Just in case I've got it wrong."

"You won't have." She looked at him expectantly, her heart skipping a beat as she realised again just how amazingly gorgeous he was. If his present to her turned out just to be a kiss, it would be fine by her. Just being able to spend time with him was amazing, and even after the six months they had been together, it was still just as magical. She smiled at him. "I really, really love you."

"Well, I was rather banking on that." Adam reached behind him and picked up a small item. He held it tightly in his hand and then, never taking his eyes from Olivia's, he slowly sank down onto one knee beside the bed and held out the small box. "Olivia Marshall, I love you more than words can possibly say, and I want to spend the rest of eternity with you. So, please, will you do me the honour of consenting to be my wife? Will you marry me?" He opened the little box and revealed a beautiful ring set with a large sapphire and two small diamonds.

Olivia stared at him and the ring and felt her whole body go light. Her head began to spin, and she leaned back against the pillows. "You want to marry me?" She finally managed to whisper. "Me?"

"Well, you are the only Olivia Marshall here." Adam grinned at her. "Are you being a bit slow on the uptake again? Yes, I want to marry you. You and no one else. And this is an engagement ring."

Olivia sat up and swung her legs out of the bed. She squatted down on the floor in front of him and stared him in the eyes. "Yes. Please. Of course I'll marry you. I can't think of anything I'd rather do."

Adam took the ring out of the box and gently slid it onto her finger. "Thank you. Thank you for making me the happiest man in the world. And happy birthday." He leant forward and kissed her on the lips.

She put her arms around his neck and held him tightly. "I love you so much," she whispered, her lips still pressed against his. "And I will love you for ever."

A word about the author...

Rachael Richey writes Women's Fiction and Romantic Comedy. She lives in Cornwall, England, with her husband and teenage son.

You can visit Rachael's website at:
http://rachaelricheybooks.weebly.com/